Bill Smith

Giddy Up,

Barney

FIRST PRINTING JUNE 1997

ISBN 0-89826-077-9

Printed by
Publishing & Printing Inc. — Knoxville, Tennessee

ACKNOWLEDGMENTS

I am extremely grateful to my lovely wife, Marian, who has allowed me the freedom to spend countless hours over the past few years getting information down on paper. She has also been very supportive.

To my oldest daughter, Faye Porcella, for urging me to get started on the book, for her encouragement along the way, as well as helping to critique my work in the final stages.

To Russ, Faye's husband, for giving unselfishly of his computer expertise and technical support.

To my younger daughter, Yvonne Stobart, for the many long hours at the computer, pounding out page after page of material. Her tireless labors have made what seemed like a huge undertaking become attainable. I am also very thankful for her patience through much indecision on my part.

To Ed, Yvonne's husband, for allowing his wife the freedom to spend so many hours away from her normal household duties.

Finally, to all my brothers and sisters for their words of encouragement and support. I consider myself blessed to be a part of such a caring family.

CONTENTS

Prologue / 9

PART ONE   1924 - 1928

Chapter 1- An Exciting Adventure / 19
Chapter 2 - White Pine Scents / 22
Chapter 3 - A Ride With Big Brothers / 24
Chapter 4 - Preschool / 27
Chapter 5 - The Blue Cloud / 29
Chapter 6 - Aw Shucks / 31
Chapter 7 - A Midnight Surprise / 33
Chapter 8 - Poison Cukes / 36
Chapter 9 - The Clover Mill / 38
Chapter 10 - The Little Red Sweater / 40
Chapter 11 - S-c-r-e-e-c-h / 42
Chapter 12 - School Daze Beginnings / 50
Chapter 13 - Tracks On the Clean Linoleum / 54

PART TWO 1928 - 1931

Chapter 1 - The Rickety Door / 59
Chapter 2 - The Hay Scene / 61
Chapter 3 - Wild Critter / 64
Chapter 4 - The Tasty Early Apples / 66
Chapter 5 - Rocks and More Rocks / 68
Chapter 6 - The Three Musketeers / 71
Chapter 7 - What Brakes?! / 74
Chapter 8 - Sleigh Ride / 76
Chapter 9 - The Storehouse / 80
Chapter 10 - A Jolt In the Night / 85
Chapter 11 - A Disappearance / 89
Chapter 12 - Slowpoke / 91
Chapter 13 - The Dreamer / 92
Chapter 14 - The Record Half-Mile / 94
Chapter 15 - Whee-e-e-e / 96
Chapter 16 - Strains From the Stable / 99

PART THREE 1931 - 1937

Chapter 1 - Winter Nightmare / 105
Chapter 2 - Our Heritage / 111
Chapter 3 - Nothing Stays the Same / 113
(A Glimpse Into the Future)
Chapter 4 - Flying Low / 115
Chapter 5 - Holiday Times / 117
Chapter 6 - Tricky Sisters / 119
Chapter 7 - Family Times / 120
(A Flashback)
Chapter 8 - Under the Pile / 123

Chapter 9 - Eerie Sounds of Night / 125
Chapter 10 - Hazards of Growing Up / 128
Chapter 11 - Mossbacks / 131
Chapter 12 - The Flea Swatter / 135
Chapter 13 - High School On the Lighter Side / 137
Chapter 14 - Fond Memories / 143
(A Flashback)
Chapter 15 - Over She Goes / 146
Chapter 16 - A Run For Cover / 151
Chapter 17 - Brown Eyes / 154
Chapter 18 - Made In the Shade / 156
Chapter 19 - Timber-r-r-r-r / 161
(A Flashback)
Chapter 20 - Sweet Smells of Silage /164

PART FOUR   1937 - 1944

Chapter 1 - Deer Tracks / 169
Chapter 2 - Lost Hunter / 180
Chapter 3 - Excited Forest Ranger / 184
Chapter 4 - Gloomy Clouds of War / 189
Chapter 5 - Tattered Tent Roof / 194
Chapter 6 - Just Who Was That Beauty? / 197
Chapter 7 - Blackouts / 201
Chapter 8 - A New Beginning / 203

Will and Susanna Smith's wedding picture

Prologue

NOTE: I have taken the following information from the copyrighted collection of Susanna Dettweiler Smith's writings.

One beautiful autumn day a lovely teenage girl with long wavy hair moved about waiting on tables for the hungry threshing crew in the Dettweiler home. Who would have ever dreamed that someday she would become the mother of thirteen children? Her name was Susanna Dettweiler. Susanna had three sisters: Magdalena, Lavina, Lillian and one brother, Elden. Susanna was next to the oldest, and, as she and her older sister moved about from kitchen to dining room with platters of food, fresh off the large wood cook stove, she seemed to be attracting a good bit of attention.

There happened to be a handsome young man there in his early twenties, who was seated at the far end of the table. Young Will Smith would snatch glimpses of her out of the corner of his eye all during the noon meal that day. But as he finished eating that big slice of homemade pie and was getting up to leave with the rest of the threshing crew, he found it almost impossible to get his mind off that beautiful girl.

So as everything in this life has a starting point, this was the beginning of what was to become a wonderful lifelong relationship as husband and wife.

William, born on December 21, 1882, on a farm near Colwood, Michigan, in Elmwood Township, of Tuscola county, was the son of Charles and Mary Dillion Smith (first child in a family of three sons and three daughters) and the grandson of John and Melissa Smith and Edward and Bridget O'Grady Dillion.

Susanna, daughter of Israel and Lydia Wideman Dettweiler (second daughter in a family of four daughters and one son), granddaughter of Henry and Matilda Dettweiler and Henry Lichty and Barbara Eby Wideman, born August 10, 1888, on a farm near Akron, Michigan. At thirteen years of age, her parents purchased a 120-acre farm one mile east of Colwood, Michigan. After moving there she attended the French Town School.

William, known as Will, and Susanna were married on January 9, 1907, at the Evangelical United Brethren parsonage in Caro, Michigan. According to Susanna, on the day they were married it took them three hours by horse and buggy to drive from Colwood to Caro because of the poor roads--a distance of only seven miles!

Happily married, Will and Susanna began housekeeping in a log house on a 40-acre farm near Colwood. Other buildings included a corn crib and granary, and to help them get off to a good start, Will's Pa gave him a cow and two pigs. Two horses came with the farm, and Susanna's Pa gave them a cow and 24 chickens.

The week following their wedding, Susanna went to the Colwood store (then owned by Claude Andrews) to buy items for their house. She purchased the following: one washboard, two washtubs, one wash boiler, clothesline, clothespins, butter bowl and ladle, bread tins, pie tins, bake pans, fry pans, kettle, tea kettle, tea pot, coffee pot, eggbeater, potato masher, wooden spoon, and Queen Anne soap. The total cost was less than $10.00!

Will worked part-time making cement blocks. He enjoyed this type of work, so he had a desire to have his own block machine. Soon after they were married, he heard that there was one for sale in Belle Isle, Michigan.

Fortunately there was an excursion by train planned for business people in August of that year, and Will and Susanna decided to go. Money being a little scarce that first year of marriage, Will borrowed $5.00 from his mother for the trip.

Boarding a train in Caro early one morning, they arrived in Detroit around noon and caught a ferryboat over to Belle Isle. Susanna had taken along some bologna sandwiches, and finding a city park they sat on a bench and ate their lunch. During their stay in town, they experienced their first automobile ride, a seven mile tour around Belle Isle for a total cost of 50 cents.

Early in the afternoon they went over to the cement works. Will found the block machine (which typically was hand operated) and made arrangements for them to ship it to him. Also included were 300 boards to be used in drying the cement blocks.

Before heading home, they decided to visit Will's Aunt Kate Crowley and her family, who lived in Detroit. They had supper with them and then boarded the train for home. Arriving in Caro the next morning about 2 o'clock a.m., they picked up their horse and buggy at the Ten Cent Barn (which got its name because of the cost per day for boarding a horse). Two hours later they were home.

The first job with his new machine was a barn for Melville Graham, who lived one-half mile south of the Colwood store. Will not only made the blocks but also laid them. Since Susanna enjoyed being outside, she was able to help him with the farm work as well as helping make the blocks.

On June 10, 1908, their oldest son, Alvin Charles, was born. In the fall of that year they moved onto a 120-acre farm and into a log house one-half mile east of Colwood.

Will and Susanna both had a desire to honor the Lord in their marriage, so very early they became involved with the Colwood United Brethren Church and established a family altar where, as a family, they could read the Word of God and pray together each morning. Alvin recalled later that the first place they took him was to church. It has been proven in the years that followed that the Lord honored that commitment.

Elden Thomas, their second son, was born, January 5, 1910. During that summer they began some improvements on their new farm by building a cement block addition to their log house and a new granary.

May 25, 1911, Roy James, their third son, was born. While he was still a small baby, Susanna fell down the stairs with him and injured his head quite seriously, which caused him much trouble later in life. During this year they built a new barn and silo. The following winter, in the midst of a very severe snowstorm, the *Detroit Free Press* reported that a country schoolteacher kept the children all night and in desperation, burned the wood from the desks in the heater to keep the children warm.

Their oldest daughter, Mabel Katherine, was born on August 22, 1913. Because of the excessive rain that year, they told of having to pull one field of navy beans by hand because it was too wet to get into the field with the bean puller. Susanna said that she and Will pulled beans until 5 o'clock in the morning to keep from losing them. The iron-wheeled wagon they used to haul the beans out of the field sank almost to the axle. That summer Will also hauled baled hay on a wagon over to Colling to be loaded onto freight cars for shipment to other cities.

December 7, 1914, their fourth son, John Orland, was born. The family had been using a single buggy for transportation up until then. But because of the increase in the family, they decided to get something with more room. Will purchased a surrey and a team of young horses, which was a real luxury in those days--comparable to buying a Cadillac today. That year they also built a chicken house out of new cement blocks that Will and Susanna had made.

Mary Ellen, their second daughter, was born October 4, 1916, and when she was eighteen months old, the house caught fire and burned down. Alvin gave an account of what happened:

Will was working on Clyde Rhodes' farm getting a field ready to plant sugar beets. While Susanna was churning butter, Alvin had gone out to the granary to get some beans for supper. On his way back to the house, he noticed the roof was on fire. In just a short time the house burned to the ground. When Will came home from work and saw what had happened, all he said was, "Well, no one was hurt, and we can build a new house." For a while the family lived in the granary and a small shed. Shortly after that Will's Pa offered him his tenant house to live in until a new house could be built.

Just recently Alvin related another incident that happened during the period of time that they lived in that tenant house.

Our folks had a hired a teenage girl, named Twilla Robinson, to help with the house work. Alvin and Elden, who were about seven and nine, were playing out in the yard in the vicinity of the outhouse at the time Twilla was making one of her trips out there. Being a bit mischievous their little wheels started turning.

They waited out of sight until she got inside and locked the door. Then quickly and quietly they grabbed a chunk of a big fence post and propped it against the outside of the door.

When she tried to open the door and couldn't, she surmised who the culprits were. Then did she ever cut loose describing what she would do if she could ever get her hands on those fellers. The boys finally did go and release their prisoner, and she promptly went and told Pa what happened.

As Pa attempted to apologize for his mischievous boys, he had a little trouble keeping a straight face. Imagine those model Smith boys pulling a prank like that!

While living in the tenant house, their third daughter, Rosella May, was born on October 23, 1918. By the time Rosella was six weeks old, they moved back onto the farm and into the new house Will had just finished building.

Soon after this Will began to get his heart set on a nicer farm a couple of miles from there. So in January 1920, he and Susanna sold that farm and bought another 120-acre farm from Alfred Kerridge, one-half mile west and one-half mile south of Colwood. He also bought a new Samson tractor, a plow, and a spring-toothed harrow to be used on the new farm. On October 27, of that year their fourth daughter, Ruth Fern, was born.

Susanna recalled that in all her married life this was the first time they had a hired man who boarded himself. It was customary before this for him to live in with the family.

August 9, 1922, their fifth son, William Jay (Bill) was born. Susanna said that at this time seven of the children attended the Remington School, and Ruth and William were the only ones home. Her health was not too good at this time, so she was glad when the older children came home from school to help with the work. She had always milked the cows and taken care of the chickens, but now some of the boys were old enough to take over these chores.

On October 19, 1924, Pearl Loretta, their fifth daughter, was born. This year Will bought a new Model "D," John Deere tractor, which was used for much of the heavier farm work.

Fred, their sixth son, was born on October 1, 1927. They were having some trouble with drainage on the farm at this time, so Will tiled most of it. This was done by a big machine which went through and dug trenches about three feet deep the full length of the field and about fifty to sixty feet apart. Four-inch clay tile were then laid in them and tied into a six-inch line at the end of the field, so as to carry the water off into a drainage ditch and out into the Saginaw Bay.

On May 26, 1929, their seventh son, Richard Edison was born. During this year their son, Roy, underwent a very serious, but successful operation at the University Hospital at Ann Arbor. It was to correct the head injury he had received as a baby when Susanna fell down the stairs with him. It was a day of great rejoicing and thanksgiving when they were finally able to bring him home. We all joined in singing, *"Hail, hail, the gangs all here, what a happy New Year"*.

In the year 1930, Elden graduated from Caro High School in June, and Donald, their youngest child, was born on December 5th.

On the following page you will find a family photo from the early '30s. Standing from left to right: Mary, Roy, Elden, Alvin, John, Mabel, and Bill. Seated from left to right: Rosella, Fred, Pa, Richard, Pearl, Ma, Donald, and Ruth.

Part One

1924 - 1928

One

An Exciting Adventure

I'm Bill, and I would like to have you return with me and experience life back on the farm, beginning in the early 1920s.

I suppose it must have been during the last year or so that Ma was alive that I related something to her that I remembered as a child. When I began to share it with her, she said, "Bill, you couldn't have been over 2 years old!" Now I don't know how it's possible for something to be impressed on our minds at that age, but she said I had described the following incident just as it happened.

The bright summer sun was peaking up over the horizon, shooting its rays through the sprawling limbs of the three white pines out in front of the big, red brick farm house. Pa went to the garage and backed out the 1921 Dodge in preparation for the long trip, while Ma was busy getting Pearl and me ready (Pearl was the baby).

Several days earlier, Pa had asked Ma if she would like to go and visit her Grandma Dettweiler who lived with Ma's Aunt Susanna Switzer. Ma said, "I sure would." The Switzers lived approximately one hundred and twenty miles west of us near Vestaburg, Michigan.

At last the day had arrived. Pa filled the car with gasoline from the fifty-five gallon drum at the back end of the workshop and took the hand operated tire pump and made sure the tires were all up good because the roads would be gravel all the way.

My older sisters were putting away the breakfast dishes as Pa came into the kitchen to get the picnic basket that had our sandwiches, homemade oatmeal cookies, and jug of drinking water for the trip. He also packed a can of tire patching, a tire pump, a small box of tools including a lug wrench, screwdriver, and a monkey wrench.

Ma had us all ready and was feeding Pearl as Pa came back in to get himself cleaned up and ready to go. In a short time, he said, "Well, let's get loaded up." I'm not sure how many of us went on this trip, but I know one thing, we were all excited and ready, because we younger ones had never taken a long trip like this before.

We all climbed into the car. Ma had Pearl on her lap in the front seat, and the rest of us kids were in the back. Pa reached in through the car window to turn on the ignition key, pulled out the choke button, and raised the spark lever on the steering post. He then walked around in front and grabbed onto the big crank that extended out from the front of the motor underneath the radiator. Two quick turns and the big motor roared a hearty response, kicking out a cloud of black smoke at the tail pipe.

As we pulled out of the driveway that morning, I was filled with excitement and pleasure for being included in such an adventure. Our trip took us through such towns as Caro, Saginaw, Breckenridge, St. Louis, and Alma. About halfway between Saginaw and St. Louis we pulled into a country schoolyard and, under a big maple tree, we spread out a blanket on the ground and sat around to eat our picnic lunch.

We arrived at Aunt Susanna's about 1:30 p.m. The Plymouth Rock chickens scampered out of the driveway where they had been dusting themselves. Cousin Oscar's big collie, with tail wagging a welcome, mosied out to greet us. Some of us young guys were strange to him--but not for long.

Oscar and his brother, Harvey, saw us drive in and came from the barnyard to escort us into the big, white frame house. As Harvey opened the front door that led into a large living room, we all filed in behind Ma and Pa.

I was immediately impressed by the age of my great-grandma Dettweiler, who sat in the far corner of the living room, needlework in hand slowly rocking in her big chair. She and Aunt Susanna were both dressed in the usual Mennonite fashion with long-sleeved black dresses, high-buttoned shoes, and their silver hair done up in a bun.

How glad they were to see us! As Aunt Susanna shared with my folks the things that were happening with them, Ma and Pa had to again name all the children and give the approximate ages of each one beginning with Alvin and right on down to Pearl and me.

After a while I became a little restless, so I decided to do some exploring around the large farm house. Pushing the screen door open, I was attracted back out to the beautiful, white porch that ran the full length of the house. The top of my head was about even with the railing, and I suppose I may have spent the next hour or so crawling in and out between the little two-by-two upright posts. That was lots of fun!

The evening meal of mashed potatoes, roast beef, gravy, stewed carrots, fresh baked bread, strawberry jelly, and apple pie for dessert finished out a wonderful day.

Because of the lateness of the hour, Pa and Ma decided not to return home that night. What an enjoyable time we had that evening laughing and telling stories. The next morning, after getting up early to a big farm breakfast, we expressed our thanks for the wonderful hospitality and all climbed into our car and headed back home.

Two

White Pine Scents

The following summer, a short while before wheat harvest, Pa and Ma began planning for another trip west. But this time, instead of a visit to relatives, it would be to attend the annual United Brethren camp meeting at Carson City, Michigan, about 110 miles away. Pa spent some time briefing the older boys on what needed to be done around the farm while he would be away, since we were getting close to grain harvest.

Overhearing the folks talking about Grandma Borroughs got me a little curious. It so happened that they had invited her to go with us to camp meeting. Oh, she wasn't really my Grandma. She was the mother of Harry Borroughs, whose family was Ma's neighbor years ago when the Dettweilers lived near Akron.

Knowing that I would celebrate my third birthday while we were at camp on August 9, she had to bring a gift along for that occasion. On the morning of the ninth, as we gathered around the little make-shift table in our big 8 x 12 tent, she handed me a small beautifully wrapped package as they all sang "Happy Birthday."

Eagerly I began tearing away at the paper and opening up the little box. Inside was the most beautiful gold-colored pocket watch engraved with a locomotive on the face and attached to a nice long chain. She thought little William was somebody special, and I really treasured that watch. In fact, I wouldn't mind if I still had it stored away with my other keepsakes.

It was so much fun being at camp, playing out under the stately white pines in my little sand pile. With a little imagination I can still almost smell that clean, strong pine fragrance that permeated the air. I don't remember much about the meetings, but I sure enjoyed hearing those beautiful church hymns, accompanied by the old pump organ drifting across through the woods. Baby Pearl, who was just beginning to walk, also shared in my sand-construction projects. With my little tin shovel and bucket, we created some pretty impressive landscape, complete with mountains, tunnels, and highways.

As I continued to grow, life seemed to become more exciting with each passing year. Of course, there were times of difficulties and disappointments, but for the most part I think our family weathered the storms pretty well. I guess I've always tried to live life to the fullest, and that being the case, it seems that I usually found myself where the action was. Sometimes that was good--and sometimes not so good.

Three

A Ride With Big Brothers

I enjoyed riding on a tractor or in a truck. One morning, probably about the middle of April, 1926, when I was too young to be of much help on the farm, my oldest brother, Alvin, asked me if I wanted to go with him to deliver a truckload of peas.

One of the early crops we raised was field peas. When the crop was ready to harvest, we would go into the field with a horse-drawn mower. The machine cut a six-foot swath, and in back of the cutting bar there was a buncher. A buncher was a series of iron slats that were shaped so as to roll the vines into a nice tight windrow behind the mower. We would then come along with the truck and pitch the vines up onto the rack. A hay loader, which was hauled along behind the truck, was sometimes used for loading peas.

Our truck at that time was a Model T Ford, probably about a 1925 model. It had a hinge-type rack which could be tipped up so the load would slide off the back. Just behind the cab there was a lever that would slide into place to hold the rack down until you wanted to unload. It was counterbalanced so when you pulled the lever back, it would take very little effort to flip the load off.

Well, we got all loaded up, and Alvin and I headed for Caro to the canning factory. Going south on the Colwood road, there is one long hill known as "Beechers Hill." We were cruising right along, probably all of thirty miles an hour, and, from where I sat on the passenger's side, I could see the hot exhaust manifold through the loose fitting floorboards. To keep my bare feet from getting burned, I pulled them back against the seat. The manifold was now turning an orange-red from the intense heat of the little four cylinder motor as it strained under the heavy load. Alvin then pulled the high speed lever back, and with the gas lever on the steering column wide open, he stomped his foot down on the low speed pedal.

Evidently, because of the extreme vibration, the lever that secured the rack slid out of place and, as it did, the big load reared up and flipped out onto the road. What a mess! Alvin, who usually was prepared for emergencies, had a pitchfork along with him. After securing the rack again, he began pitching those tangled pea vines back up onto the truck one weary forkful at a time. Fortunately, there was very little traffic on the road, so before long we were back on our way into town.

At the factory, the vines were run through a process that shelled the peas from the pods, then the vines were conveyed up onto a big stack outside the building. After a few weeks time, the vines would go through a fermenting process and then were sold back to the farmers as silage for the cattle. The shelled peas would be washed, graded, and sealed in cans, after which they went through a cooking process. The cans were then labeled and packaged for shipping to grocery outlets.

Lima beans were handled about the same way, except instead of cutting them with a mowing machine, they were pulled out of the ground, roots and all, with a bean puller. They were also picked up with a pitchfork or hay loader, and then hauled to the canning factory.

Pa and my older brothers did some custom hauling with our Model T truck. One afternoon my brother, Elden, ask me to go with him to get a load of lima beans out near Fairgrove. I was always game for a ride, and as I remember it was late in the evening when we got our load on and headed out for Caro.

By the time we got onto the road it was pitch dark. We were coming into town from the west with the gas peddle slap-dab to the floor board when something went, "THUMP!" The truck shook a little, so Elden eased off on the gas peddle and looked for a place to pull off the road. By the time we got stopped, there was the angry motorist glaring in at us with his beady eyes straining through the tangled bean vines that hung down over the window.

The problem was that our load was so large that the vines hung over the truck rack and obscured our tail lights. This young man with his girlfriend had come up behind us in a '30 model Ford roadster with the top down and slammed into the side of our load. The impact sprung the post on the right side of his windshield and gave them both quite a scare. I was too young to remember how things were settled for the damage, but I was old enough to remember that Elden and I were pretty well shaken up!

Four

Preschool

It was the summer of 1926, and in just a few weeks I would be old enough to start grade school. My first few years I had a wonderful teacher, whose name was Edgar Hodges. Really, my initial introduction to school happened the year before I officially began. I was four years old, and I guess my sisters, Mabel and Mary, wanted to show me off. So they took me one day as a visitor. Wow! That was so much fun, getting all that attention and seeing all the exciting things that happen in that one-room schoolhouse.

They had all eight grades in one room, which was approximately thirty-eight feet wide by forty-eight feet long. There was a girl's cloakroom on the left side at the back, and the boy's on the right. Each of these rooms had hooks along two walls for hanging overcoats, caps, etc., and a row of shelves down one side for lunch boxes. In the classroom, there was a recitation bench across the front where each grade would assemble for their lessons. With five or six in each group, they would take turns coming up for their class. Starting with the primers, the teacher would work his way up through the eight grades. Each class lasted about 45 minutes to an hour. Total enrollment for a school year may have been an average of 40 to 60 students.

Each student had his own single seat-desk combination with a shelf underneath for extra books and papers (and other important things like rubber bands--used for extra-curricular activities!). The desktop had a long groove for pens or pencils. On the right was a glass inkwell for dipping your ink pen. There was a blackboard all the way across the front of the room. In later years, I saw it close-up, because that was the corner where the kids stood for punishment who caused mischief. I can't imagine why they picked on me!

When the bell rang that first morning, all the kids began to file into their seats, and my sisters had me sit right down on the very front row. It so happened that a whole row of seventh and eighth grade girls sat right directly behind me. As a child I had blond curls that had been let grow quite long, and wouldn't you know it, those girls (Mae Dillon, Charlotte Hyde, and I don't remember who else) kept bugging me by running their fingers through my curls. Yuk! Too bad I hadn't been about ten years older, but by that time the curls were all gone!

That was my introduction to the Remington School.

Five

The Blue Cloud

I soon became old enough to do some small chores around the house, so Ma would have me carry in wood for the big cookstove. This stove also burned coal. I would take the coal scuttle, getting as much as I could carry and set it at the end of the stove next to the wood box. This stove, or range as it was also called, had a water reservoir on one side. It held about ten gallons of rainwater that was usually carried from the cistern pump in the washroom. When it was kept full, there was always an ample supply of warm water on hand for washing clothes, mopping floors, etc.

Ma had a two-cycle Maytag gasoline-powered washing machine. Before washing she filled the gas tank with gasoline mixed with oil. While she was getting the motor ready to run, the big ten-gallon copper boiler was on the wood cookstove full of rainwater being heated for the wash. At the side of the machine was a bench holding two large washtubs full of rinse water with the hand-crank clothes wringer between them. When the water on the stove was hot enough to use, she had one of my older sisters help her carry it out on the porch to be emptied into the washer. Next, a few shavin's of lye soap was tossed in with the first load of clothes.

She closed the lid and, holding the choke lever down, stepped on the starter. About the second time over, "Bang! bang! bang!" Even if you couldn't hear the washer, you could tell it was washday by the big cloud of blue smoke ascending out from under the low porch roof.

On the farm our only source of light was either kerosene or gasoline lamps or lantern. Kerosene was a little safer to use, so I suppose we used kerosene more than gasoline. We usually kept a little gallon kerosene can handy for use in filling the lamps and lanterns.

One evening after supper Ma asked me to go to the woodshed, which was just a few steps from the back door, and fill the little can with kerosene. It was stored in a 55-gallon drum, set up on sawhorses, laying in a horizontal position. When the barrel was pretty full all you had to do was turn the spigot and fill up your container. But this particular time the barrel was getting down low enough so that the fuel wouldn't run out without tipping the barrel forward. So, with the can in my left hand, I grabbed hold of the top edge of the barrel and pulled forward. When I did, the fuel rushed to my end, and over the barrel came, sawhorses and all, falling forward with the fuel running all over me. I was pinned down getting wetter by the second. I yelled for help and one of my sisters came running out and rolled the barrel off from me. I wasn't hurt much, just drenched with kerosene--and plenty scared!

Six

Aw Shucks

We had two buildings in which we kept laying hens, usually white leghorns. My job was to feed and water them and gather the eggs. What a thrill to reach into the nests and pull out those big white eggs! It wasn't uncommon to carry in a 10 - 12 quart basketful every night. Because of our large family, we used quite a few, but there was usually some extra each week that Ma saved up to trade for groceries at the country store.

My Pa's sister, Aunt Kate, owned the store at that time, so we bought most of our groceries, shoes, clothes, etc. from her. She had a special attraction there on Saturday nights. For an added incentive to get people into the store, she sponsored a horseshoe tournament. As many as 16 men could play all at one time, which was quite exciting. My brothers, Roy and John, played on the team. Although I was much too young to play myself, there was something I could do; keep score. She offered an incentive for that also. The pay for keeping score was a double-dip ice cream cone with 5 dips, so I tried to make it each week. Pa would quite often go along and play checkers inside the store with John Matt, Sam McCreedy, and some of the other older men.

I enjoyed having Pa along because he would usually buy a big sack of shuck peanuts to take home. Coming into the big dining room, he would set them on the table and by the light of the kerosene lamp we would all enjoy our fill. To make it even more of a treat, one of the girls would bring in a couple of dishes of homemade butter and set one of them at each end of the table. As we all sat around shucking and eating peanuts, we could reach over and dip one end of the shucked peanut into the butter before eating it. Mm-mm good. I could go for a sackful right now. The floor would be a mess when we finished, but it was worth it. A few minutes with the broom and dust pan put us right back to normal again. That was always a highlight of the week at our house.

Seven

A Midnight Surprise

It seems that most of the exciting things during my first five or six years were times spent with my older brothers or my Pa. One such experience with Pa I will never forget. Many times after a long hard day's work in the field, he would have some work in the blacksmith shop that needed to be done, repairing farm machinery or building some piece of equipment. Our source of light in the shop was either a kerosene or gasoline lantern.

I don't know whether I felt sorry for him working out there all alone or whether I was just interested in what he was making. Many times I found myself out there with him until the wee hours of the night holding the lantern so he would have his hands free to work. Some of the time I would also turn the crank on the blacksmith forge.

A forge was a piece of coal-burning equipment that was used to heat up pieces of iron so that it could be hammered or bent into the proper shape. There was an air blower underneath that fanned the flame, so it would heat the iron hotter. I enjoyed seeing a piece of iron turn from a gray-black to a white-hot. At that point it could be shaped almost any way you wanted it by a few clips with the hammer on a blacksmith anvil. A big pile of scrap iron along the side of the toolshed came in handy when Pa needed a piece of iron for his projects.

On one bitterly cold day in mid-January we had butchered several hogs. The meat had all been cut up and the fat cubed to be processed into lard. This was sort of a long drawn out ordeal. The cubes of pork fat had been put into the large cast-iron lard kettle. The kettle was suspended over a hot bed of coals, usually built of hardwood. After the fire got going real good, someone would have to stir the fat around in the kettle with a wooden paddle every thirty minutes or so. This generally lasted several hours into the night. Either Pa or one of my older brothers usually took care of it. This particular night Pa said he would watch the lard kettle, so I ask him if I could stay up with him.

We had the kettle set up right in front of the toolshed, which also provided some protection from the bitter cold north wind. Pa and I each found a big block of wood for a seat and folded up a few burlap bags for a cushion.

I loved the smell of the pork fat cooking along with the homey scent of hardwood smoke swirling out from under the big black kettle. With the orange-red glow bouncing off those big oak logs, we just settled down next to the fire with our coat collars turned up to shield our ears from the night air.

I wasn't much for initiating a conversation, but enjoyed the company of my Pa. We just sat quietly for an hour or so. Occasionally, Pa would take the wooden paddle and stir the fat around to keep it from scorching the bottom of the kettle. Then without saying a word to me, he got up from his stool and walked back into the toolshed, which was all open on the end toward the lard kettle. He began getting some pieces of one-inch hardwood lumber down from overhead where he had it stored.

He cut the boards about four and a half feet long, and took a coping saw and cut little carved out pieces on one edge of each one. Then he took a plane and a draw-shave to round off the edges of the boards on one end. I didn't have the slightest idea what he was making until he started hammering out metal runners for one edge of the boards. Around midnight, with the orange glow of the fire under the lard kettle reflecting back into the tool shed, Pa put the finishing touches to a brand new hand sleigh. He picked it up off the workbench, walked out to where I was, and handed it to me. Words can't express how I felt at that moment. It was beautiful!

Over the next several years that sled hauled wood for the cookstove, feed for the hogs, ten-gallon milk cans full of milk, not to say anything of the many rides for all of us kids on the snow and ice.

I will never forget one such ride. It had snowed all night and Pa was going to take us kids to school with the old Buick. He asked me if I would like to ride to school on the sled behind the car. Like a dummy I said, "Sure!" I tied the sled rope (which was probably about 5 feet long) to the rear bumper of the car while the other kids (Rosella, Ruth, Pearl, and Fred) all got in with Pa. Then pulling my stocking-leg cap over my ears, I climbed onto the sled securing my books and lunch bucket. Pa started up the old Buick, circled the garage, and headed south past the apple orchard. We hadn't gone far when I realized that I might have made the wrong choice. When he slowed to turn the corner down by the big dredge cut, I scooted right under the back bumper. You know, you can get hurt that way!

Now, down the final stretch one-half mile west to the school, we whizzed past Uncle Forest's old place and on we went lickety-split. I was glad I had my ear-loppers down over my ears 'cause it was sure breezy. I think he must have forgotten that I was back there because the snow, gravel stones, and dust were creating a mini blizzard around my face all the way there. After that ordeal I decided that walking to school wasn't such a bad idea after all!

35

Eight

Poison Cukes

When I was about six or seven, Pa worked for the Clarke Canning Company. He was a field man, and the company furnished him with a nice new 1929 Model A Ford pick-up. I can almost see him now, backing that shiny black beauty out of the garage on his way to work, proud that he had been chosen for that important job. I believe he liked his work, because he enjoyed meeting people. His work was to go around to the farmers in our area who had contracted to grow peas or lima beans for the Clarke Company. He would keep check on what stage of ripening the crops were in and advise the farmers as to when they should start harvesting.

I was in grade school at that time. Going to and from school, I walked with two neighbor boys, Frank and Nick Sherbine. One afternoon on the way home, Frank spotted a field of cucumbers over on Clarence Donahue's farm just off the road a few yards. We noticed that there were quite a few yellow overripe cukes laying on the ground.

Frank said, "Hey, let's go get some to eat."

"I don't know about that," I answered warily, "my folks say that those yellow ones are poison."

They both chimed in, "Naw, we eat 'em all the time."

I said, "Okay, if you're sure."

We crossed the big road ditch and sneaked out into the patch, which was partially obscured by large bushes, and each got a big, fat yellow cucumber. Without peeling or slicing it, we just sat down and started gnawing away on our prize. I was expecting any minute to begin getting stomach cramps or something worse. But about that time, I thought I was hearing a familiar noise. It sounded very much like my Pa's company pick-up. Sure enough, I spotted it through the willow hedge-row near the road ditch.

I said to the guys, "I've got to get out of here." So, dropping my treasure, I beat it over to the road ditch and hid behind the trees until Pa rounded the corner and headed toward home. Fortunately, he hadn't seen us, and I never let it be known what we had done, 'cuz I didn't want to get *those guys* into trouble *(A-hem)*.

But I can tell you a little secret, yellow cukes aren't poisonous. However, I guess sometimes kids are just going to be kids, but I don't recommend going against our parents wishes, because things don't always turn out so rosy.

Nine

The Clover Mill

During the summer months, one of my jobs was to tend the cattle in the pasture. It would not necessarily be the same field each year. Alfalfa and sweet clover were typical crops for grazing milk cows. After breakfast each morning, I would put on my little straw hat and head out the back door. In a split second, our old faithful dog Collie (pronounced with a long o) was at my side. He was probably a cross between a Bernese cattle dog and Border Collie. (Incidentally, Bernese cattle dogs are a Swiss breed, and some of our ancestors came from Switzerland.) I would go to the barn and turn the fourteen milk cows out of the barnyard and follow them barefooted back down the dusty lane to the pasture.

I didn't mind watching them, but I did get a little lonesome out there by myself. So, to pass the time away, I decided to build a little mill for grinding clover stalks. Finding a large, flat stone and another smaller one that fit into my hand real good, I went around breaking off big handfuls of clover and alfalfa stems, putting them in a little pile.

Now it was time to start grinding. I sat down on the ground with the flat stone between my legs, then with the smaller stone in one hand and a handful of clover in the other, I would go at it. You should have seen that beautiful, bright green clover pulp, and juice running over the side of my mill. As you can see, it didn't seem to take too much to amuse me back then. At least I think I have a little better appreciation of how Moses felt while he tended sheep on the backside of the desert those forty years.

Often I would bring the cows back home at noon. It was fun following them down the lane, shuffling my bare feet along in the wagon tracks. I can still see the big, fluffy clouds created by the powdery dust of the white clay, stirred up by my bare feet scuffing along. The only hazard to this fun was the danger of little sharp stones that may be obscured beneath the loose surface. They could give even tough feet a nasty cut.

Ten

The Little Red Sweater

Along about the last of April 1927 as the frost was beginning to come out of the oat stubble fields, Pa pulled around in front of the barn with Doll and Floss on the manure spreader. As he started back down the lane, I hollered and asked if I could go along with him. He said, "I don't see why not." Really, there was not a good place for a passenger to ride on the spreader. So, I sorta had to squeeze onto the iron seat with him.

Before I continue with my story, let me give you a little description of a manure spreader. It was shaped similar to a long narrow wagon with sides about twenty-four inches high, with an endless conveyor in the floor called an apron. When in gear, the conveyor would move the load of manure little by little to the rear of the spreader, where it came in contact with whirling beaters. These were about twelve inches in diameter with spikes for tearing the manure apart, before throwing it out onto the ground. There were two levers along side the driver's seat; one for engaging the apron and the other for throwing the beaters in gear.

When the spreader was nearly empty, I slipped off the seat and just stood behind him on the floor. Evidently, he

40

had his mind on other things as we headed back across the field toward the barn, so forgot to disengage the beaters and the conveyor apron.

I guess I must have been dreaming also and was not aware of the fact that I was being slowly but surely moved back, inch by inch, toward those whirling beaters. The wooden floor being so wet and slippery, you couldn't feel your feet sliding along. I was standing sideways and didn't realize what was happening until one of the beater tines grabbed the sleeve of my new red sweater, and almost tore it off my back. I yelled, and Pa stopped just in time to keep me from being pulled right into those nasty beaters.

Alvin had been riding the tractor nearby, and told us later that he was seeing what was happening, but because of the tractor noise couldn't get our attention. I wasn't hurt much, just a few bruises on my arms, but it sure tore up my nice new sweater!

Eleven

S-c-r-e-e-c-h

As we walked down the lane past the big wheat field on our way to hoe beans in the summer of 1927, there were signs that it wouldn't be long before harvest time. The heads of grain had tinges of brown and yellow in them as they swayed back and forth in the late afternoon breezes. We had this twenty acres of wheat just back of the barn, ten acres of oats on the north side of the lane, and twelve acres of barley next to the woods across the road from Howard Remington's place.

Since grain harvest was just around the corner, Pa and my brothers began making plans for it. Alvin and Elden harnessed up Dan and Floss, hitched them onto the old McCormick Deering grain binder, pulled it out of the back shed, and brought it around in front of the workshop. They unhitched it and went on to other things as Pa and I went to work on the binder.

First of all, we disconnected the cutting bar which had a series of teeth that were angle-shaped. We had a large grindstone out next to the silo that was used for sharpening tools. While I cranked and kept a little water dripping on it, Pa sharpened the cutting bar. The water kept the sand washed away so it could do a better job of sharpening. In a short time we had the binder back together and all greased up ready to go.

This machine cut about a five-foot swath. The stalks of grain would fall back onto a canvas conveyor and be carried up and over into a compartment on the outside of the machine. There it was packed into measured size bundles. At a set time, a long circular needle came over the bundle of grain and tied a string of binder-twine around it. As soon as the knot was tied, another couple of arms were activated that whirled around from underneath the bundle, and kicked it out onto the ground. While all this was going on, another bundle was being formed and so on around and around the field, until the grain was all cut down.

The next step in the process of harvesting was what we called "shocking the grain." The bundles of grain would be laying all over the field. The size of the field could range from 5, 10, or 20 acres. Since it was not a good idea to leave the grain lying on the ground exposed to the weather too long, it would have to be shocked up.

The normal way to do this was for a person to go through the field picking up the bundles one at a time, putting one under each arm with the heads of the grain in front of them. He then set them down facing each other with the heads up. Next, he would get two more and set them right up against the first two, and so on until he had as many as six to eight bundles facing each other in each shock. He would go throughout the field until it was all set up in shocks.

The purpose of setting the grain up this way was so the heads of grain would be up off the ground in case of rain. The bundles in each individual shock would settle together and tend to shed the rain. With normal weather conditions, grain could be left in shocks for many days without any harm.

As the Michigan summer days stretched out about to their limit, with the long fields of corn about shoulder high and the navy beans getting too big and bushy to cultivate anymore, we knew that autumn was just around the corner.

To make it even a little more autumn-like you could hear the rooster pheasants early in the morning as they screeched out of their roosting place in the big maple tree and sailed off to hide under the lush sugar beet leaves. They loved to eat on the crown of the beet plants. During harvest time you could always find an occasional beet with little holes pecked in the crown next to the leaves. By the way, that would be a favorite place to hunt come October 15th!

By this time, Pa and our neighbors began to get a little anxious about threshing the grain before it was exposed to too much wet weather. Our nearest neighbor to the north, Roy Vader, had just finished shocking his grain a few days earlier. Pa got in touch with him and two or three of the other close farmers to make plans for calling in the man with the threshing machine.

There was probably one threshing machine (grain separator) for every ten to twenty farmers. The man who owned the machine would quite often schedule the jobs so he could go right from one farm to the next, until he had the whole neighborhood covered. The normal custom was for five or six farmers in a given area to work together, until they each had their threshing done.

For instance, when it was our turn to thresh, Pa would contact all the close neighbors who were cooperating in our group: Roy Vader, Uncle Tom Smith, Uncle Charlie Smith, Uncle Forest Vader, and Clarence Donahue. The man who owned the threshing machine at that time was Hiram Kelly from Colling. His hired man's name was Elmer Connant.

In my mind's eye, I can visualize the whole scene. Pa and the older boys had spent most of the day before getting the barn floor cleaned off, the granary bins cleaned out, and rat holes patched with pieces of tin. The next morning, as soon as breakfast was over, everyone got busy getting the horses harnessed and both wagons ready. We had one high wheeled and one low iron wheeled wagon. We put Prince and Barney on one, and Dan and Floss on the other. A short time later there appeared the occasional puff of black smoke over in the vicinity of Donahue's tenant house, as the big machine came into view.

To a little feller, this was an exciting time! One of the things that helped to make it exciting was the fact that this particular machine was powered by a huge steam engine. This engine was about twice the size of the average tractor, and before they had rubber tires, so you could hear the big machine coming, grinding along over the gravel roads.

It also had what Mr. Kelly called a wildcat whistle. His usual custom was to cut loose on that silly whistle right out in front of our house and, if you weren't expecting it, it would scare the living day-lights out of you. All of us little guys would get pretty jittery as we anticipated his arrival. Well, at last our waiting was over.

We were beginning to hear the loud racket of the heavy iron wheels in the loose gravel. Looking through the apple orchard, we could see him over on the Cass City road near Uncle Forest Vader's. Pa and the older boys cleared the yard of cars and trucks to make plenty of room. Hear it came, puff, puff, clang, clang as Mr. Kelly guided his big machine along in front of the house.

Just about the time he passed the two crab apple trees at the corner of our front yard, Rosella, Ruthie, and I scampered upstairs and made a dive under the beds to drown out some of the terrible racket. And, sure enough, scre-e-e-ch as he reached up and pulled the lever on that miserable whistle.

When we thought it was safe to come out, the girls would go downstairs, and I would casually go to the window facing the barn, and watch them position the big machine right at the barn entrance in front of the drive floor. After they got the grain separator positioned, they blocked the wheels so it would stay put.

Next, they backed the steam engine out away from the separator, approximately seventy-five feet. From that position, the separator was powered by a heavy leather belt, eight to ten inches wide and about seventy-five to eighty feet long.

Now, since this was a steam powered engine, rather than burning gasoline or diesel fuel, it burned wood or coal. Instead of a fuel tank, it had a firebox much like a wood or coal furnace. But then it also had a boiler. The boiler was a long, round tank, laying horizontally above the firebox, and the boiler had to be kept full of water. As the fire in the box got hot enough to heat the water in the boiler, steam would be produced, and only then would you have power to run the grain separator.

They usually brought along a water wagon, which was either a truck with a big water tank on it or a horse-drawn wagon. By bringing water with them they were always assured of plenty, regardless of where they set up the machine. Now the engine was fired up and ready to begin threshing grain. Big clouds of coal smoke began belching out of the smokestack.

Just a little description of the grain separator. Its overall length was probably twenty-five to thirty feet long. At the back end, it had what was called the blower pipe. It was a large, galvanized pipe about twelve inches in diameter, approximately fifteen feet long, with an adjustable elbow at the outer end. There was a large fan at the base of the pipe, and as the grain straw was carried back through the machine, it fell into a big fan, and was blown up through this pipe and out onto the straw stack.

While these two men were getting their machine set up, several others were out in the field with their horses and wagons loading up grain. The neighbors, who brought their team and wagon, also furnished extra help. The men drove through the fields with their wagons, while one man walked along side pitching the bundles up, the other arranged them neatly on the rack.

The first wagon to be loaded would head for the barn. By this time the threshing machine was running with the big leather belt slapping against itself. Mr. Kelly would turn on the steam, and they'd be ready to begin threshing grain.

The man who had driven his team and wagon up along side, hung the horses' lines over the front of the wagon, and began pitching the bundles of wheat into the front end of the machine.

Remember, we said the wheat was tied with binder twine. At the very front of the machine was the feeder. As the bundles of wheat were thrown into the feeder heads first, they began to be carried back, right into the throat of the machine. Here there was a series of sharp knives that cut the twine, so that the sheaves of wheat could loosely move right on into the cylinders, where the heads of grain were torn free from the straw. Then, through a set of shakers and blowers, the nice clean kernels of wheat were sifted down into a compartment, where they were then augured up into a bagger. If it was a good crop of wheat, it usually required at least two men to handle this operation.

The bagger was a gadget where two grain bags hung on a spout. As the one bag became full, the lever was flipped, and the other bag began filling up. While that one was filling, the first one was carried back and emptied into the granary, and so on all day long. While this process was going on, the straw and light chaff was being shuffled and moved back to the rear of the machine. Here it spilled off into the big fan to be blown out onto the straw stack.

As the sun began to sink in the western sky, it became evident that we'd soon be done for the day. Apparently dampness moves in before the sun actually sets and toughens the grain to the point where it does not separate properly. The man operating the machine could tell when that happened, because his big machine groaned whenever

47

a bundle of wheat was thrown in. At this point, he would motion for them to stop feeding in the bundles. As soon as the machine had blown out the straw that was in it, Mr. Kelley would shut down the steam engine, and all would be quiet again.

The men then unhitched their teams from the wagons and secured them near a little pile of hay while they went into the house for supper. There could be anywhere from twelve to sixteen men to feed at one time. Threshing was a dusty job, so instead of all those men coming right into the house to wash up, Ma would have some of us kids fill a large washtub with water out in the yard. That way, the men could just dive in without worrying about spattering up the floors.

Ma and my older sisters could really serve up a scrumptious meal. Mashed potatoes, gravy, chicken, beef, maybe ham, homemade bread, with pie or cake. Of course, us little guys had to wait for the second shift, but it was always worth it.

Sometimes it would take more than one day to do all of our threshing, so the entire crew would come back the next morning. As soon as our grain was threshed, they would all move on to the next neighbor on the list. When the steam engine pulled out of our yard, instead of a spot of oil in the driveway, there was a pile of ashes. It was then our family's turn to furnish a team of horses and wagon and an extra man, either Pa or one of my older brothers. How wonderful it was to experience the teamwork among this group of neighbors--something we don't see much of these days.

My how quiet it was after all the machinery and wagons had pulled away. It was also a good feeling to have the granary again bulging with wheat, oats, and barley. The cattle sure enjoyed frolicking around in the nice fresh straw that fell down around the run shed back of the barn. We kids enjoyed it, too, although we weren't supposed to climb up around the stack until it got settled into place, which took a few days after threshing.

That new straw also had other uses besides being used for bedding the livestock. Ma couldn't resist getting all of us kids involved with refilling the straw ticks. In case I've lost some of you younger ones, I'll try to explain. Straw ticks took the place of mattresses on our beds. You might say it resembled an oversized pillowcase filled with straw. It was the size of the bed and made of cloth called ticking. It was a tough blue and white striped cotton material, which would be opened up and refilled with new straw at least once a year. I guess all of us got involved in that process at least a few times as we were growing up on the farm.

During a house cleaning spree, Ma would have the older girls pull all the ticks off the beds, unstitch one end, and put them on the porch. Then us younger guys and gals would grab one by the top, drag it out, and dump the old straw on the barn floor. We would then all join in with two of us holding it open, while a couple others scooped up armfuls of new, clean straw and filled it up again. Oat straw was usually chosen for this purpose because wheat and barley had sharp whiskers on the heads. With one of us at each end, we carried them carefully back and set them on the back porch, where the older girls would again stitch them together. It sure was a nice feeling to crawl into bed on top of a big, fluffy tick full of clean new straw!

Twelve

School Daze Beginnings

I really enjoyed my first few years in grade school. It was a one-room brick building called the Remington School on the corner of East Cass City and Remington Road. (Named after the Remington family who lived nearby.) For the first three years my teacher was Edgar Hodges. I learned to read well and sound out words very early. He was an excellent teacher and was very patient with all of us.

My best friend those first few years was Richard Colley, the son of Jay Colley, who was president of the Colwood Bank. By the way, my middle name is Jay, named after Jay Colley.

School would let out for Richard and me an hour or so earlier than for my older brothers and sisters. So, to pass the time away, we would go to the basement and sit on the steps and read stories aloud out of some of the old out-dated readers, such as the *Story Hour Reader*. We got along just fine until one of us began to giggle, then the teacher would have to send someone to quiet us down.

One winter around the first of the year, Mr. Hodges asked Pa to come with his gasoline engine and a pump-jack so we could flood the schoolyard for ice skating, hockey, etc. Pa connected the jack up to the deep-well pump out in the front of the school under the big maple tree and just left it pumping all day long. Can you imagine trying to study inside that old schoolroom, while the whole east half of the schoolyard was turning into a huge skating rink? With the ground already frozen, the water turned to ice almost immediately, providing beautiful ice skating for most of the winter.

Hockey was a favorite sport for the older boys, while the younger ones enjoyed "belly flopping" with their sleds. A few days later a big northeaster blew in carrying a heavy blanket of soft, fluffy snow. The huge flakes just sifted down like big white feathers.

At school we played fox and geese for a while, and then for a change we decided to have a snowball fight between the boys and girls. There happened to be one girl that I liked pretty well by the name of Maxine. And you may not know this, but it is usually the girl you like the best at which you throw the snowballs! Well, Maxine was a few years older than I, and she wore glasses. So, to show her how much I cared about her, I packed a snowball real hard and let it fly.

Yep, you guessed it. It smacked her right on the side of the face and smashed her glasses to smithereens. Boy, was I sick! But based on past experience, I really didn't think I was *that* good of a shot. However, sometimes you just draw the losing ticket. Bless her heart, she took it pretty well, and it didn't seem to ruin our friendship. I think she knew that I wouldn't hurt her intentionally. Why do kids do such stupid things? As they say, *hindsight is better than foresight.*

The annual Christmas program at school was always a highlight. One of the things I liked about it was getting out of classes for the practice sessions. I also enjoyed memorizing and reciting my part in plays, etc.. A few days before the program, Pa or one of the close neighbors would bring the big tree, usually a ten to twelve foot cedar, and the seventh and eighth graders would get to decorate it. From then right on to the night of the program, it was difficult keeping our minds on schoolwork. When the big night finally arrived, we had a great time. But what a mess after the little boxes of hard candy, chocolate drops, and shuck peanuts were all sampled! There was a great stir of excitement as the little folks tore open their gifts, scattering paper, ribbons, and bows high, wide and handsome.

Monthly parent-teachers meetings were a special time also. Everyone was welcome--children as well as parents. They often had special singing, storytelling, or drama. Lola Remington and Jesse Hyde occasionally sang duets.

At one of their meetings, the teacher at the Sunshine School asked Roy and John if they would put on something special for their next PTA. The boys decided to get up a little orchestra and invited two of our cousins to help. Roy played the harmonica, John the banjo, Harold Goudie the guitar, Merrill Goudie a Jew's harp, and I dressed up as a black lady and danced while they played. I don't know how much the people enjoyed it, but we sure did!

On warm days at school there were a variety of fun activities during recess. Softball was a favorite as well as shooting darts. These darts were not the kind that you shot into a dartboard. They were homemade ones. We took a wooden cedar shingle and whittled the thick end down to a point with a notch cut just in back of the tip. The thin end of the shingle was left wide enough to serve as a tail. Then we cut a strong piece of rubber band and tied a string double to one end of it. At this point, we were all ready to go. We hooked the string loop into the notch, held the rubber band in one hand and pulled back on the tail of the dart with the other hand. It was very important to make sure that it was pointed straight up, before letting her fly. Knowing how critical these next few moments were going to be, we stood breathless. It was not uncommon for those little rascals to come up missing momentarily, before making their mad rush back toward Ol' Mother Earth.

Now you also want to make sure that you are out of the way! One unlucky guy, Bob McRae, had his come down and stick into the cloth top of the teacher's 1931 Plymouth sedan. I can still remember the sick feeling, seeing nothing but about three or four inches of the dart tail visible above the roof of that beautiful car! Thank goodness those kind of deals were the exception and not the rule. I know one thing, our fun sure came to a screeching halt for that day.

Thirteen

Tracks On the Clean Linoleum

Although most of my time during those early years was spent with Pa and my brothers, I also had five wonderful sisters: Mabel, Mary, Rosella, Ruth and Pearl. First of all, I want to say that I appreciate their patience with me during those growing up years. Being somewhat of a tease, I must have tested them to the limit and, as we all know, that can be easily overdone.

I remember the time I came in from the barn and found Mabel busy mopping the kitchen floor. The chairs and tables were all off to one side, and the woodbox and coal scuttle were moved into the washroom out of the way. Now, I don't know yet why it seemed to be so much fun sneaking across the wet linoleum, but I just had to have some cookies or something out of the cupboard. I hurried so as not to leave any tracks on the sparkling floor, as if hurrying would help.

Lo and behold, Mabel was watching for me, and before I knew what was happening, I was being ushered out the back door with the help of a wet mop. Did you ever get slapped in the back of the neck with a wet, soapy, dirty floor mop? Oh, oh, "sloptic dote"! (See note on the bottom of page 56.) By the time the kitchen door slammed shut, I had cleared the first three steps with a handful of cookie crumbs in my fist.

Probably some of the most memorable times with my sisters were on a Sunday afternoon or an evening after work. Often, the older girls would go into the kitchen and begin stirring up a pan of fudge, or maybe pop some corn. Taffy was another favorite. Several of us would get in on the taffy pull. They usually would make a large batch of it to feed our whole crew. When it was ready to take out of the pans, the candy was sort of a light tan color and very gooey. At this point, it wasn't quite ready to eat. It had to be pulled first.

Most of us kids wanted to get in on the taffy pulling. This was done by picking up a chunk about the size of a softball, pulling it in both directions, wadding it up, and stretching it out over and over again. After several minutes of this treatment, the ball of taffy would change to a light ivory color. Next, we would flatten it out into strips, 10 to 12 inches long by 1 1/2 inches wide. We then laid them out on top of the snowbanks along the back porch. In a short while they would be nice and brittle, just right to hold in our hands and lick.

All of the girls were a great help with the housework, as well as helping out in the fields. For many of those years, Ma, as well as the older girls, had their hands full, caring for the little ones.

Much of the farm work was shared by all the members of our family. For several of those years, Rosella, Ruthie, Pearl, and I worked side by side thinning sugar beets, hoeing beans, and corn.

Some of you might be interested in the seating arrangements at our table. We usually ate all our meals in the kitchen, except for very special occasions which were enjoyed in the large dining room. As you might expect, the kitchen table was quite long, maybe eight or ten feet. Pa sat at the head, with Ma on his right, and Alvin on his left. The other three older boys sat down the left side, and the older girls down the right side next to Ma. That would be Alvin, Elden, Roy, and John on Pa's left, and Ma, Mary, Rosella, and Ruth on Pa's right. Mabel and I sat at the far end on a bench. At that time Pearl would have been the baby and probably was in the highchair between Ma and Pa.

Note: Our mother, Susanna, being of Pennsylvania Dutch background, spoke Dutch. They had a slang saying similar to one of ours. When someone really upsets us, we might jokingly say, "I'll knock your block off!" Sloptic dote is a Dutch version of that. Sloptic-- meaning, "I will strike you." Dote--meaning, "dead!"

Part Two

1928 - 1931

One

The Rickety Door

The Remington School building was built of red, clay brick, and in back all the way to the property line (approximately 125 yards from the school building), were two outside toilets also of brick construction.

One day my good friend, Bob Grice, and I decided to pay a visit to the boys' toilet. I don't know why, but it seemed the normal thing was for us to race to see who could get there first. But what neither one of us knew was that our teacher, Mr. Hodges, was already seated in there when we arrived.

We were headed down the final stretch at full throttle, and as luck would have it, I got there first. Instead of slowing down and opening the door like normal people, I had to plow into it with both hands!

It was one of those wooden doors that had inset panel sections. My two hands hit right against the middle panel, pushing it out of the door and into the teacher's lap, splinters flying every which way! Now mind you, Mr. Hodges was a huge feller with dark brown eyes, heavy black hair, and thick bushy eyebrows. Imagine our chagrin as we peered through this, our newly created, "bench-level" window!

This much I remember: I had a terrible time explaining why I was so careless, but that was not the worst of it. My friend, Bob, told the teacher that I had, on a previous occasion, thrown a roll of paper down the toilet hole.

Now all this trouble in itself would have been serious enough, but what I hadn't told you was that if any of us received a whipping at school, we would also get one when we got home. My penalty was to bring a switch to school the next day. So, the next morning on the way to school, I broke off a small branch from the crab apple tree at the corner of our backyard and reluctantly carried it to school. (That was a shame, marring that beautiful tree.) Sure enough, when I arrived, I followed Mr. Hodges to the basement for my lashing. It wasn't as bad as I expected, just a few smacks across the back of my legs, but I do remember it.

And, you guessed it, I also got one when I got home. That was one thing about my Pa--he was not slack concerning his promises.

Two

The Hay Scene

I had always looked forward to school vacation. Even though it meant lots of hard work, it was still a good change. We raised a lot of hay on our farm, so during the hay cutting season there was always something for all ages to do.

Driving any kind of motorized equipment was something I really enjoyed doing. One summer Pa had more hay than we needed for our own use, so he began selling it right from the field. We had one customer come from Colling who had bought hay from us before, and we knew him pretty well. His name was George McCreedy. George had a huge Reo Speed Wagon truck with a long rack for hauling loose hay.

During this time we were using a hay loader. This was a piece of equipment that could be pulled behind a wagon or truck, and it would pick the hay up out of a windrow and convey it right up on top of the load. That way, all you had to do was stand up there and arrange it around with a pitchfork.

The hay was already raked into big windrows. We just drove the truck along straddle the windrow, and it ended up on top of the truck. But someone had to drive the truck along nice and slow. Would you believe that Pa ask me if I would like that job? I suppose I was six or seven then, and I didn't waste any time climbing up into that monster. Wow, what a machine! I had never seen so many levers and buttons in my life. It looked like the cockpit of a P38. But of course, all I had to do was steer it straddle the windrow of hay.

One of the men would put it in creeper gear for me, then jump out, and leave me on my own. I could just barely see over the dash by looking through the spokes of the big steering wheel. Another neat thing was the long gearshift lever, which had a large marble knob screwed onto the end of it. It was white with orange marble-like swirls mixed all through it. Wow, what a beauty!

Another one of my jobs was to drive the horses on the high-wheeled wagon in the hay field. The wagon had what we called standards on each end of the wagon. These were like ladders about six or seven feet high that were used to help hold the load in place.

I stood up as high as I could on the front standard, usually barefooted, and drove old Prince and Barney along straddle the windrow of hay, so it would feed directly into the loader. One of the older boys took the hay from the loader and arranged it with a pitchfork. Occasionally, I would get a good dose of hay chaff or thistle barbs down my neck, which didn't add to the enjoyment. When we got all the hay on that would stay, we unhitched the loader and took our wagon to the barn.

Since the hay was going to be put in the mow or loft, we had to have a way of getting it up there. There were different methods of unloading this loose hay off the wagon, both requiring a team of horses or a tractor hitched to a hay rope. You could either use a set of slings or a pair of hayforks. We generally used the hayforks.

I'll try to explain how it worked.

There had to be a long, one-inch diameter rope strung through a pulley at the base of the front barn door. It continued up through a series of pulleys into a mechanism that rolled along on a track the full length of the barn. It then came back down, double to the barn floor, or in this case, to the load of hay. The double rope had a pair of pulleys with iron hooks on them. Someone on the load of hay would set the two large hayforks down into the load, hook the two pulleys to the forks, then holler down to the driver, and give him the go ahead. The team of horses hooked to the big rope would start pulling until the hay was up high enough to clear the big cross-timbers.

At this point, the car on the track then carried this big bunch of hay across into the mow. When it was over the right spot, a little trip rope was pulled, the two forks would release their load, and down it would come. There was always at least one man in the mow to distribute the hay around, while the man on the load would be hooking into another bunch. This went on until the wagon was empty, probably about four trips with the double forks. It was fairly common to have one of the rope slings on the wagon floor for the last trip up. Later on we used a small tractor or car on the hay rope.

In a normal year, we would have enough to fill the hay mows on both ends of the barn; alfalfa over the cow stable, and timothy over the horse stable.

Three

Wild Critter

One prayer meeting night everyone had gone to church except Mabel, Pearl, Fred, Dick, and I. Dick was the baby and not feeling well, so Mabel said she would stay home with him, and I guess we stayed to keep her company. I must have been six or seven at the time. All went fine until we began to hear some strange sounds coming from the south side of the front porch.

The next thing we knew there was a loud bellering and pawing of hooves in the flowers just outside the living room window near the asparagus bed. It was no mystery as to what was going on. The bull had gotten loose and was letting the world know. Needless to say, Mabel and all of us younger ones were pretty scared.

We didn't think he could get in the house, but on the other hand, we weren't sure that he might not be bold enough to try a door or window. There was no phone at the church, so we called our neighbor, Roy Vader. He went over to get Pa and our older brothers. It wasn't long before they were all out there with shovels and pitchforks trying to round up that big bruiser. They finally got him corralled, but not before he got himself in trouble.

It was customary then to keep a big brass ring in the bull's nose for the purpose of tying or leading him. Well, it seems that this silly critter, while on his rampage, got his nose-ring caught in a cast-iron silo filler blower that was laying in a junk pile along side the toolshed. While the men were trying to close in on him, in his fury, he just threw his head back and flung the blower up and over his shoulders. As he did, it jerked the ring out of his nose.

I need to mention here that the blower probably weighed about one hundred and twenty-five pounds. Of course that infuriated him all the more, and he went storming around the yard. Finally, the men, with their forks and shovels, were able to get him back in the barn. Wow, what a night that was!

Four

The Tasty Early Apples

School vacation had now become a little less exciting with all the hoeing of beans, sugar beets, and corn in full swing. Fortunately, we would get a little break from the routine whenever those warm weather thunder showers popped up.

One afternoon we had just gotten into the bean field and started across when we began to notice the clouds thickening up over the Rutledge's barn. (Our storms usually came in from that direction.) Now and then we saw a small flash of lightning, and then almost out of nowhere, BOOM! That was our clue to beat it to the house. We had heard of people being struck by lightening working in the fields and none of us wanted to be caught staying out there too long.

Racing happily down the lane toward the house, we could see the white sheet of rain moving in from the west with the strong winds beginning to sway the tall corn back and forth. Dashing into the yard, we scampered up the concrete steps into the kitchen just as the first big drops began to pound on the porch roof. We hoped the rain would last all afternoon.

All safely inside, we slouched down in chairs around the big kitchen table to regain our strength by devouring a nice thick slice of homemade bread loaded with brown sugar and cream. The rain kept coming down in torrents, and we could begin to hear the fresh rainwater as it came rushing through the downspouts into the big cistern in the basement.

As the sky began to clear and the rain had almost stopped, all of us kids prepared to bolt out the back door to the Astican apple tree next to the smokehouse. These were the small, red early apples that we looked forward to every summer. The heavy rain had knocked about a dozen off onto the ground, and we each scooped up two or three on our way to the barn to get a chip off the ol' salt block to flavor our apples. It was about mid-afternoon by then, so we were still able to get in an hour or two of hoeing beans.

Five

Rocks and More Rocks

From the time I was old enough to help with the farm work at all (which was around six or seven years old), my job was not driving a tractor, but a team of horses. We had one big tractor, 1923 Model D, John Deere, for the heavy work such as plowing, etc., but most of the other work was done with the two teams of horses we had. I didn't especially like having to drive horses. In fact, as strange as it may seem, I didn't care about riding them either.

One of the jobs I cared the least about was driving Prince and Barney on the float. A float was built out of heavy planks. We took about five, 2 x 10s that were twelve feet long and spiked them together so that one overlapped the other. When it was finished, it was about four feet wide and twelve feet long. We fastened a clevis to each end and attached a long chain to them. The horses pulled from the middle of the chain. The float was used for leveling the ground and breaking up hard clods of soil.

It also had another function. On our farm there were plenty of stones, and each spring there would be a fresh crop that had worked their way up to the surface of the ground. So part of my job was to pick them up as I went across the field with the float. Many times I wouldn't know a stone was in front of me until the float bounced over it, almost pitching me off. Then I'd have to stop the horses, pick up the stone, and load it on the float. At the end of the field, I would have to stop and unload them along the fence. Doesn't that sound exciting?

Well, it did get a little exciting one day for a few minutes. We had two teams of horses at that time, Maude and Tony, and Prince and Barney (all Belgiums). This particular day I was driving Price and Barney. These two horses were about as opposite as it is possible to be. Prince was very high-strung and fast, and Barney was slow and easygoing. I had them on the float in the big field back of the barn and had come up to one end. I stopped and unloaded the stones, then proceeded to turn the horses around.

"Giddy up, Barney," I yelled. (I didn't need to speak to Prince. He was always ready.) Barney was on the left and I was turning them left. Instead of them both stepping right out to make the turn, Barney lagged behind just enough so that the left end of the float got stuck under one of his hind feet. That caused the other end of the float to rear up off the ground. When it did, Prince got spooked and surged ahead. With that, he flipped the float completely over end ways.

This all happened so fast I didn't quite have time to make it out of the way before it came crashing down. The end of the float caught the right side of my knee and knocked me flat! With considerable squirming, I was able to pull myself free and get up without any broken bones. But I did receive a long bruise down the side of my right leg. After a few choice words for Barney, and with a little tugging and straining, I was able to get the float right side up again.

As I got a little older, I was promoted to doing some cultivating with a team and our Plant-It Junior, a one-row cultivator. That was more of a challenge, as well as a lot more fun. I especially liked cultivating corn after it got up about twelve inches high. The horses followed right along

69

nicely between the rows, and I just sat there and steered the cultivator wheels with a foot bar. At the end of each row, I would reach up and pull the lever back, lifting the gangs up out of the ground for turning. This was a nice change from trudging along behind on foot. Time went faster, too.

Six

The Three Musketeers

"Come on, Bill," yelled Roy. "Bring the five-tined fork from the cow stable and help us clean out this pen. John will be around with the horses and spreader in a few minutes."

As I slipped on my rubber boots and started out the back barn door with my fork, I heard John holler, "Whoa, Prince," as he pulled the team of beautiful Belgiums around behind the big straw stack.

We three guys usually had the job of cleaning out the bull pen. This was not a job that any of us looked forward to because, as we have seen already, bulls have been known to get a little ornery at times. The bull pen was stuck out in the barnyard partly covered by a big stack of straw. The back and both sides of the pen were under the stack. The front of the pen was enclosed with a big heavy beam, which was a 6 x 6 timber suspended about two and a half feet above the ground. As you might expect, the accumulation of straw and manure under him would build up quite a bit over a period of time.

All of us were pretty brave when the bull was on one side of the fence, and we were on the other. I suppose we even bragged about what we would do, just in case he got loose.

We seemed to be getting along fine that day and had already taken several loads out into the field, but a strange thing was happening of which we were unaware.

As we continued to dig out the manure on the front side of the pen, the space between the beam and the ground was getting greater. Finally, after finishing out another load, John left with it, and Roy and I disappeared into the barn. (Strange as it may seem, we just might have been teasing the ol' feller along through the day.) We had no more than left him alone until he decided that there was now room to walk out under the beam. So, out he came!

While John was back in the field spreading the load of manure, I had gone through the barn and on to the house for something when I thought I heard somebody holler. I looked back, and there was Roy leaning out through a crack in the big barn door. He had already realized the bull was on the loose and was checking to see if the coast was clear in front of the barn so he could race to the house. I yelled out to him that the bull was nowhere to be seen, so he decided to make a run for the chicken house for the first leg of his trip. But on his way, he encountered bad luck. Rounding the lower end of the chicken house, he banged his head on the corner of the roof and was knocked out cold. As he laid there sprawled out on the ground, the bull circled around that end of the barn and raced right on past, apparently not even seeing Roy.

All this was happening up around the buildings without John being aware of any of it. But as he started back toward the barn with the team and spreader, the bull spotted him, and ran out to greet him. Luckily, there was a fence between John and the bull. Not wanting to take any chances, John jumped off the spreader, leaving his horses standing there, and headed for the house on the dead run. It so happened that on that side of the fence, there was also a lean-to hog pen with a long sloping roof that went all the way to the ground. John, with coattail flying straight out, went sailing right up to the peak of the roof and jumped off into the tomato patch on the other side. From there, he beat it for the house.

While we were all getting quieted down, the bull was working off some of his excess energy running up and down the field behind the barn. After the initial shock of the episode, we gathered up some long-handled shovels, and with fear and trembling, began to coax him back into an enclosure until we were able to make his pen more secure. We were all thankful that no one was seriously hurt. Poor Roy suffered the most with a lump on the head!

Seven

What Brakes?!

It was getting along late in the afternoon on one of those hot summer days, and all of us guys were sort of weary from pulling weeds out of the navy beans. John said, "Come on, Bill, let's go get the cows." Really, it didn't require two grown boys to bring the cows up from the pasture, but I think he wanted to make it a little more exciting since we were all about bushed.

As he cranked up the doodle bug, I climbed up on the passenger side. I must mention that this was a strange little machine. It had a Model T Ford motor and two Chevy transmissions. In low, the little rascal would go so slow you could barely see it move. But in the highest gear, the slowest it would go was around twenty-five miles per hour. To make it a little more interesting to drive, the transmissions both had to be in gear in order to have any brakes.

Now, let me explain the setting for this next scene. Pa had just recently built and installed a brand new Basswood gate in the lane that goes back into the fields. There was a short stretch of driveway past the toolshed, then it turned toward the lane. The gate was just around the corner about one hundred yards, and CLOSED! Gravel stones flying, we rounded the corner and there stood the gate. But instead of slowing down and easing up to it, John was going to sail right along, then hit the brakes. That would have been fine, except that one of the transmissions had jumped out of gear, and we didn't have any!

Would you believe we hit that gate going about twenty-five miles per hour? We rode right up onto it and down it went in splinters. Maybe you think we didn't have a time explaining this whole episode to our Pa. But, of course, that was not the first time, nor would it be the last, that he had to come along behind and pick up the pieces for some of us guys.

Eight

Sleigh Ride

Winters on the farm were fun for the most part. Oh, there were always some things not so pleasant, like having to do the chores night and morning, rain or shine. But there was still plenty of time for fun things, especially when there was snow on the ground. We did get some pretty big snows at times. It was not unusual to have snowdrifts as high as the fences along the road.

Much of the winter the ponds and creeks were frozen over, making it ideal for skating. Many times on moonlit nights or Sunday afternoons a group of us kids would put on our woolen or sheep skin coats and stocking-leg caps as we dashed out to the ice ponds. The skates clamped right onto the soles of our regular shoes. They had an adjustment for the length and a small key for tightening the clamps that held them onto the soles. Our times skating were great fun, even if we were cold, wet, and covered with snow when we came in.

Now and then we would get a big snowstorm on the weekend, so much that it would be almost impossible to get out with the car. One Saturday evening as we carried out the last can of milk into the milk house, we could see that the storm clouds were forming off in the northwest skies. As we all sat around in the warm dining room later that night, we began to hear the driving snow as it beat against the north side of the house. The snow must have kept coming down all night, because when we went out Sunday morning to do the chores the drifts were piled three to four feet high. It looked like we might be socked in for the weekend. Pa and Ma were not much for calling off going to Sunday School and church, so Pa said, "We'll take the horses and sleighs."

Off to Sunday School

After the chores were done and breakfast over, Alvin and Elden harnessed up Doll and Floss and hitched them to the big sleighs. They covered it with a layer of straw and drove the team around to the front of the house. Then they gathered up all the wool blankets they could find for everyone to wrap up in. With our stocking-leg caps, heavy overcoats, scarves, and galoshes, we climbed aboard, and off to church we went in style.

The fluffy, white snow sprayed up over our blankets as we breezed right along, and in no time at all we were pulling into the church yard. Folks who had to depend on cars that day, didn't make it to church. That was a fun ride even though it did take a little time getting thawed out after we got there.

In addition to the sleighs, we also had a one-horse cutter to use when there was snow on the ground. It was similar to a buggy, except instead of having wheels, it had runners that glided along smoothly on the snow. Being a fairly light vehicle, we stored it over the drive floor of the corn crib during the summer months. It had probably been a few years since we had gotten it down to use. One winter Sunday afternoon Roy and John decided they would like to take a ride in that cutter. So a few of us lifted it down from the loft, and they hitched ol' Tony up to it.

The cutter had a seat with a cushion wide enough for two. Then the front was formed out of real thin plywood or composition board and was curved up high enough so that a person's feet were fairly well protected from snow or rain while driving along. It looked pretty classy, but that front paneling was not super strong.

The boys got all hitched up and started down the lane toward the back barn, which was about a quarter of a mile from the other buildings. There was quite a lot of snow on the ground, so they could not tell what might be lurking just below the surface. They climbed aboard, spoke to Ol' Tony, and off they went sailing along through the fluffy snow. One thing they had forgotten, however, was that they had to cross a ditch just before getting to the barn. Of course, the ditch was now level, filled with new-fallen snow.

Well, you guessed it. Tony jumped the ditch, but the cutter with Roy and John didn't. When the front of those big runners hit the bank, Tony broke loose from the cutter and Roy and John were thrown forward right through that beautiful paneling.

As the boys arrived back at the house with Tony dragging the remains of the cutter, I'm sure they were racking their brain, trying to decide how to break the news to Pa. I don't believe that the Smith family cutter ever flew again.

Nine

The Storehouse

"Bang," went the kitchen door when a strong gust of wintry air jerked it out of my hand as Roy, John, and I came in from doing the chores one bleak January night. We could see an occasional flake of snow bounce off the north windowpane as the kerosene lamp cast its reflection across the room. It was so good to be inside on such a bitterly cold night. While we played Carrom, the girls were in the kitchen popping corn and making candy. We could hear the tin popper as it slid back and forth on top of the wood cook stove, with the rich aroma seeping up through the holes in the lid. It sure smelled scrumptious.

As Pa got up from reading the *Detroit Free Press* he said, "You know, they are predicting several days of below freezing weather, and I believe this would be a good time to butcher those four hogs."

The mercury had really dipped by morning, and the light skiff of snow was dry and squeaky under foot as we went to the barn to milk the cows. With the chores done, all of us guys worked with Pa to get everything ready to butcher. We set a fifty-gallon wooden barrel just inside the large opening at the front end of the toolshed. Directly above the barrel was a windlass, which was used for lifting a heavy load. It was a homemade wooden hoist that I'll try to describe. There was a long, round pole about eight inches in diameter laying crossways above the ceiling joist of the shed. Somewhere near half the length of the pole, they had built a large wooden pulley about three feet in diameter. This pulley had a wide groove that would allow a one-inch rope to travel around it. In other words, there were two ropes used. One was around the pulley for leverage. The other was around the pole and hung down with an iron hook on the end for pulling up heavy loads.

To prepare for butchering, we filled the wooden barrel with scalding water. After the hogs were killed, we would pull them in and out of the hot water three to four times to loosen the hair before laying them on a table made of sawhorses and large planks. We would then take scrapers and scrape all the hair off. After this was done, the hog was hauled up again by the hind legs and dressed out. By nightfall the four hogs were all cut up and ready for processing.

Since Ma came from a Pennsylvania Dutch background, they did some things at butchering time that others may not have done.

Here's a partial list of things that were produced from a butchered hog: sausage, sugar-cured ham, smoked hams and shoulders, spare-ribs, pickled pigs feet, pickled tongue and heart, head cheese, lard, and soap.

I'll try my best to describe some of these procedures.

Lard: Before the days of vegetable shortening, most people used lard made from animal fat. This process involved cutting all the fat portions off the pork. We had a large iron kettle out in the yard with a heavy iron jacket around it to hold in the heat and also to hold up the kettle. The kettle held about fifty to seventy-five gallons. We cut the fat up into small cubes, threw them in the kettle, and built a hot fire under it. It was necessary to keep the fire constant for several hours and stir the fat occasionally. When the grease was all fried out of the fat, the residue would rise to the surface to be skimmed off. We then dipped the grease out and poured it into twenty-five pound lard cans, which we stored for use through the winter for baking and frying foods.

Soap: I wasn't old enough to remember too well, but I'll describe the process as best I can. We took the portion of the hog that was not normally used for meat, such as parts of the head, ears, feet, tail, etc., and threw them into the big iron kettle that was in the woodshed. The kettle would be heated up with a wood fire underneath, and sometime during the cooking process lye was added. As the cooking continued, the animal fat with the lye mixed in rose to the surface.

After a period of time, we let the fire die down. If it was left in there over night to cool, by morning we would have a nice, off-white colored sheet of lye soap about four inches thick and three to four feet in diameter. When we needed soap for washing dishes or clothes, someone would go to the woodshed, break off a chunk, and with a paring knife would shave off whatever was needed for the job. It sure got things clean, although it was a little hard on your hands.

Sausage: Usually Grandma and Grandpa Dettweiler, or someone in that family, had a sausage grinder and a sausage press that we could use. Sausage was made from smaller scraps of meat that was cut away from the better cuts, such as hams, ribs, etc.. The sausage grinder had a hand crank. One person would crank, while another person fed in the strips of meat.

After it was all ground up, there were at least two different methods used for caring for it. One was to form the meat into patties and process them in glass jars to be used later.

The other, which was sometime used, was to press it into links, like is seen today in the meat counter at the supermarkets. What was used for the liner to stuff the sausage into was a long portion of the animal's intestine. The long tubular-like substance would be extracted from the intestines and cleaned in a pan of water. It was somewhat stretchy and shaped like a long flexible, transparent tube about one and a half inches in diameter. The sausage would be forced into this long sleeve by using a sausage press. This was similar to a cider press, except this one had a pipe-shaped opening at the base, and the casing (as it was called) would be slipped right over the pipe outlet. One person would hold the casing onto the pipe, while the other filled the press and turned the crank. The plunger in the press would force the sausage down and out into the casing. These could be twisted off at whatever length you wanted the links.

Sugar curing: This was a common practice for preserving the hams and shoulders. I'll try to describe to you how this was done.

We ordinarily butchered several hogs at a time. In our basement, Pa had set up wooden sawhorses with long planks on them. We would bring all the hams and shoulders (I suppose twenty to twenty-four) down into the basement and lay them out in a long row on these planks.

Ma had the ingredients all mixed up for the curing process. Everyday for the next several days, one of us would go down and turn each of the hams over and rub this mixture into the surface. One day it would be the meat side, the next day, the skin side. I'm not absolutely sure about what all went into this mix, but this is close: brown sugar, saltpeter, sage, salt, and pepper. This mixture was kept in a large pan on the end of the planks.

Part of the reason for this treatment was to draw the moisture out of the meat. Whenever we turned them after they had set for twenty-four hours, the under side would be wet. The process was repeated for a given number of days (twelve to fourteen). At the end of this regimen, the meat was preserved and would keep for long periods of time.

Smoking: We had a nice brick smokehouse that was used quite often. Inside, the meat was hung about three feet above the fire on iron hooks. A new fire would be built each morning, usually consisting of dry corn cobs and covered with green apple tree wood. By the door being kept tightly closed for several days, the intensity of the smoke flavored and preserved the meat. You talk about something tasty!

Other uses for the smokehouse was for curing fish. Pa had built a rack with chicken wire, and he suspended it up about four feet above the fire. We would clean the fish and lay them up on the rack. Probably the most common fish we smoked was herring. A couple of those little dudes sure made a tasty treat in the middle of the afternoon!

Ten

A Jolt In the Night!

Pa had built a fish shanty for fishing through the ice. It was built of basswood covered with tar paper and was approximately five to six feet square and five feet high. It had a trap door in the middle of the floor that would be positioned directly over a hole that had been cut in the ice.

In the shanty, there was a tiny wood stove about twelve inches square for heating, as well as for cooking meals. Down each side was a skimpy bunk, which served as a bench used for fishing during the day and sleeping at night. Can't you just visualize yourself sitting there gazing down through the bottom of the shanty into that clear, cold water waiting for that big northern pike to come along?

Michigan weather is rather unpredictable, and the winter of 1928 was no exception. After several days of bitter cold with some flurry of snow mixed in, there began a slight warming trend, but even so, Pa was quite sure that the bay would still be frozen thick enough to hold up the truck. So, one evening after we all came in from doing chores, Pa went to the phone and called his good friend and close neighbor, John Matt, and asked him if he would like to go fishing with him in the morning.

"I sure would," he answered, "what time we leavin'?"

"I'll be along about daybreak," Pa replied.

We quite often kept the little shanty up in the hay mow just off the barn floor. We kids used it for a playhouse or hideaway in between fishing trips. The problem was that it didn't have any windows, and the only source of light was what reflected up through the hole as it sat on the ice. We would leave the door stand open so we could see to read or do coloring.

Next morning, before the chickens were up, Alvin and Elden helped Pa load the shanty onto the Ford Model T truck. They also threw on a couple of long planks (for emergencies), fish spears, ice spud (for chopping a square hole through the ice), and a chunk of light rope.

Just as the sun was breaking over the woods across the road Pa, with his heavy sheepskin coat on and a small box of groceries in his hand, climbed into the truck. Raising the spark lever with one hand and turning the ignition key with the other, there was the familiar buz-z-z-z of the ignition coil under the dashboard. Alvin, who was helping him, walked around in front, and with a couple whirls of the crank, the little four-cylinder started right up.

As Pa pulled out of the driveway, he said, "See ya in a couple of days."

Driving a half-mile north, and a quarter of a mile east, he stopped to pick up John, and off they went. Destination--Saginaw Bay, which was about twenty to thirty miles north. A few miles up the road, they had already decided in what area they would fish. In the vicinity of Bay Park, they found the little road that wound its way out to the bay. The weather began to warm up even more that day and some thawing began to occur. They found the spot they were looking for about a mile off shore. Climbing out of the truck, they each grabbed hold of the handles on the end of the shanty, lifting it off onto the ice. While John got the fishing gear ready, Pa started chopping a hole in the ice about two feet square. In just minutes, they slid the shanty over the hole and were ready for the excitement.

Each of them took a short piece of small rope, tied one end to the spear handle, and the other end to the roof of the shanty above their heads, just in case they lost their grip on the handle of the spear. Pike and pickerel were running good that day, and they were having fun. Their supper that evening, cooked on a little tiny cook stove, included fresh caught fish. What a time they were having! Since they were both sort of tired, they decided to turn in shortly after dark--even though they had a gasoline lantern along with them and could have stayed up later. It's hard to imagine these two grown men bunking in that little shanty. John could just barely get his six-foot body to stay on his bunk, but somehow when you are enjoying yourself those kinds of things don't seem to matter. In no time, they were both sawing logs.

The weather had continued warming most of the day and into the night, and they were both getting a little concerned, but I guess they were willing to take the chance on the ice holding firm. It was so quiet and peaceful out there since the nearest shanty was several yards away. Along about two o'clock in the morning, they were both jolted awake. Boom! It was like the sound of dynamite in the distance. But to Pa and John, it wasn't dynamite, it was breaking ice--something an ice fisherman hopes he never has to experience.

A big section of ice will break off and begin moving away from the main section along the shore line. So, they weren't taking any chances. Pa lit the lantern, and they frantically got dressed and loaded the shanty along with all the fishing gear. There was just no time to waste!

They climbed in, and Pa swung the truck around and headed for the shore. They hadn't gone far, with headlights piercing the eerie darkness, when John hollered, "There it is!"

Sure enough, a long, dark streak stretched out across the lake into the blackness. The ice had broken loose from the section along the mainland and was very slowly moving out to sea with at least two scared fisherman and their gear. But they knew what to do. They had come prepared. Fortunately, the crack was only a couple of feet wide, and they lost no time in pulling the two planks out of the truck, laying them over the dark chasm, and very slowly driving the truck across safely to the other side.

Much relieved at reaching safety, they spent a few minutes trying to decide what to do next. Reluctantly, John said, "It kinda looks like our fishing trip is washed up for this time, but it sure was exciting while it lasted!" Climbing back into the truck, they headed for shore and on toward home, thankful for the Lord's protection.

Eleven

A Disappearance

It was Sunday afternoon. The dinner dishes rattled as the older girls finished putting them away. Ma and Pa had laid down to take a little nap, but we younger kids were too full of energy to waste a Sunday afternoon in bed. Rosella, Ruthie, and I got our heads together and came up with a neat idea. Since the second cutting of hay was now in the barn with the mows about as full as we could get them, it seemed reasonable to go up there and do some acrobatics.

I can still see the layout of the barn. As we came in on the barn drive floor, the first level of the mow was about eight feet high. So we had to climb up a pole ladder to get to that first mow. But you see, it had about eight to ten feet of hay in it, and then back of the first mow was another level of hay, maybe ten feet above the first one. The front mow had a hole cut in the floor about three feet square, for the purpose of throwing hay down into the cow stable below. Whenever we got ready to feed the cattle, one of us would have to go up in the mow and throw hay down. As soon as we finished, we would take a big forkful of hay and set it over the hole. This kept the cold air from coming down into the stable. Now that you have the picture, go with Rosella, Ruthie, and me up in the mow to tumble around and have fun.

Since the back mow was much more full than the front one, we decided to climb up to the top of that one and, in turn, each jump to the next level below, seven to eight feet down. But what I had completely forgotten about was the three-foot square hole in the mow below with a thin layer of hay spread over it.

Ruthie was the first to jump as Rosella and I watched. Whoosh, Ruthie disappeared out of sight. Then it dawned on me--the HOLE! Too late! Bless her heart, she had gone right slap dab through that hole and on down into the cow stable below a total of about sixteen feet. Rosella and I almost flew down the ladder to get to her. Rushing through the stable door, we saw her laying there, out colder than a mackerel. Boy, were we scared! We probably weren't supposed to be out there in the first place, and then to have this happen!

Well, after a little coaxing, she roused up enough so we could get her back up on her feet again. Then, instead of going straight to the house, we checked outside to see if the coast was clear. Cautiously, we then stole our way through the backyard between the buildings, helping her over to the empty tenant house next to the orchard. We were actually stalling for time while we decided how we would explain this episode to Ma and Pa. I don't remember how we broke the news to them--if we ever did--but I do know this much, we were three scared kids.

Twelve

Slowpoke

Barney was a good ol' horse, but he was a slowpoke. During my earlier years, I spent day after weary day driving Prince and Barney, so I got extremely accustomed to saying, "Giddy-up, Barney."

One day several of us were on our way to Caro in our old '27 Buick. This was a heavy car and very slow in picking up speed. Pa was driving, Alvin was in the front seat with him, and I was sitting between them.

We had gone south to the corner and had turned west toward the Remington School, and as the car slowly gained speed I spoke up in a monotonous, out-of-habit tone of voice, "Giddy-up, Barney." Fortunately, out of the mercy of God, and because of the steady drone of the car motor, no one heard me. If they did, they kept quiet so as not to embarrass me any more than I already was; hence, the title of my book, *Giddy-Up, Barney*.

Thirteen

The Dreamer

I spent a good bit of time with Roy and John when I was between five and ten years old. We did a lot of things together: work, as well as play. Roy was a dreamer and he could come up with some of the most outlandish ideas. I'll see if I can relate a couple of them.

One of the first that I remember was an airplane. This was about the time when Charles Lindbergh made his trans-atlantic flight, so I guess the boys reasoned that if the Lindberghs could do it, so could they.

How they came up with all the parts that would go into that plane, I will never know, but they had a big stack of them stored in the upstairs of the tenant house. The three of us would work on it almost every Sunday afternoon, or I should say, the two of them worked while I watched. They used big sheets of light sheet-iron for the fuselage, and strips of plywood for the wings and tail. I don't remember what they made the propeller out of, but they planned to power it with a windup-type phonograph motor.

I can just hear somebody saying, "I can see it all now. Small plane takes off out of an upstairs window, driven by nothing more than a little phonograph motor, about the size of a softball." But like I said, Roy was a dreamer. So, finally the day came for them to try it out.

Do you want to know something? Their big test came when they tried to get their little creation out through the bedroom door. Those boys never did find out how it would fly, because they ended up dismantling the whole thing piece by piece and pitching it out the back bedroom window. But I still think that if they were here today, both of them would tell you that the fun of creating something from scratch was really what it was all about.

Another dream that Roy had was a device for helping out in parallel parking. He wanted to invent a piece of equipment that mounted on the underside of any automobile, and be powered from the car's motor. I'll try to explain what it would do. With this gadget mounted under your car, you would pull up along side of the parking space. Then, instead of the normal zigzagging back and forth, you would push a button on the dash, and this device would lower itself. As it did, it would lift your car up on a little set of dolly-wheels and slowly roll you into your parking space. Roy knew that it was workable, but like most inventions, it takes more than just having the idea in your head.

Would you believe, a few years later he read in a magazine that someone had invented a device similar to his. It must not have proven too successful, or there would have been more said about it. After finding this out, Roy felt like his idea wasn't so outlandish after all.

Fourteen

The Record Half-Mile

It must have been along about the middle of May that our church (Colwood United Brethren) began to prepare for the annual Children's Day program. This would include all ages of children and young people. As is usually the case, it takes several practice sessions to get everyone prepared for their part.

We were having our practice on weeknights. This one particular night, John and I decided to walk, and the others would come later in the car. (The church was one-half mile south and one-half mile east of our home.) We walked the first stretch and, just as we were coming up to the corner, we noticed a car coming from the west, headed toward the church. We recognized the man driving as John McNiel, a friend of our folks. John was driving an old Model T Ford and traveling his normal speed, which was about 25 mph.

On the spur of the moment John said, "Let's grab his bumper." What a mistake! Did you ever try to walk at 25 mph? I don't think the old man even saw us, but as he came by, we jumped out and both grabbed on. Well, I doubt if any other two humans have ever topped our record for the half-mile! It was sort of like the fellow that was holding onto a raccoon. His partner ask him if he wanted help to hang on and he said, "No, I want help to let go."

You see, when we grabbed the bumper we were somewhat committed. If we let go, we would have fallen face down and slid along in the gravel. So, we hung on for dear life the full half-mile stretch. We were taking steps ten to fifteen feet apart. One thing for which we were very thankful, Mr. McNiel did slow down when he came to the church corner, and we were able to turn loose. I guess neither of us ever tried a trick like that again!

This happened to be the time of year many of the spring flowers were in full bloom, and the ladies would use all types to decorate the sanctuary: yellow roses, spirea, etc.. About the second week of June was the traditional time for the Children's Day programs. It was a real blessing for the kids to be involved in sharing a witness for the Lord. They participated by group singing, recitations, and memory verses with the older ones sharing in drama. It was a fun time for everyone, especially the parents, as they watched their children take part.

Fifteen

Whee⁻e⁻e⁻e

The barn floor was a good place to romp and tumble. It was fun experimenting with the double ropes and pulleys that could be raised up and down over the barn floor. One day Roy and I were in the barn doing chores. Roy was on the left side caring for the horses, and I was on the other side getting feed out for the cows. We both happened to come onto the drive floor at the same time, and Roy had the bright idea of taking a break. So, for a little fun, he asked me if I'd like to take a ride on the double pulleys.

These pulleys were made of iron with a one-inch rope running through them. They hung as a pair over the barn floor and could be pulled all the way to the peak of the barn, which was thirty to thirty-five feet up.

"How'd you like for me to haul you up on the pulleys?" Roy asked me in a mischievous tone of voice.

Even at the tender age of about eight, I was game for a little fun, so without further thought, I said, "I guess , if you promise to let me back down when I'm ready."

He answered, "Oh, sure. You know me!" The problem was, I did know him, but I went along with it anyway.

So, I walked over to the center of the floor, reached up and grabbed onto those smooth iron hooks with all the grip I could muster. He stepped over to the side of the floor where the big rope hung down and took hold of it.

You must understand here that at the peak of the barn there was an iron car that rolled on a track, with the rope running through it. Also, hanging down from that car was a small trip rope that came all the way to the floor. The purpose of this rope was to release those pulleys and their load, in this case me. Once the pulling action stopped, that locked the pulley from going either up or down. It only moved again when the rope was either pulled for it to go higher, or the trip rope was pulled and held, to let that whole contraption come sailing down. The only way to stop this downward motion was to release your hold on the trip rope.

Now it was always a good idea to have a generous layer of hay or straw on the floor before trying these goofy games. But not wanting to be bothered with any of those trivial details, we just forged ahead.

With both of us in position, Roy yelled, "Here goes." And he wasn't kidding! Up, up, up, I went.

"That's high enough," I screamed down at him. So there I stopped, dangling about fifteen feet above the barn floor. You might be thinking that fifteen feet isn't very high, but if it's you up there and it's a bare concrete floor under you, I believe you'd think that it was high enough, too! By this time, my hands were beginning to get tired and starting to lose their grip.

Trying not to reveal my panic, I hollered, "I'm ready to come down now."

But like brothers are inclined to do sometimes, he just left me there a few more seconds. Even just a small delay can seem like ages when you're dealing with fear. With a grin on his face, he slowly reached up for his little trip rope and gave it a quick jerk.

Whee-e-e, down I came, lickety-split, with the pulleys and rope singing a merry tune. When I was just a few feet from the floor, he released the trip rope, which locked the pulleys up tight. The end result of this scenario was that the pulleys came to a screeching halt, but I continued my downward momentum.

At this point there was some good news and bad news involved. The bad news was that I came crashing down onto that bare concrete floor on my backside. The good news was that Roy, with his quick thinking, released the trip rope which kept the iron pulleys from following me all the way down and clunking me on the head. That turned out to be enough "fun" to last me for quite a while!

Sixteen

Strains From the Stable

Becoming a little older, I was promoted to milking cows. I was not especially fond of the job, but the rule was: if you were given a job to do--you did it. So, as with the many other jobs around the farm, we tried to weave a little fun into our work, such as competing to see who could finish their tasks first.

Since the next two children older than myself were girls, Rosella and Ruthie, I didn't have an older brother close to my age. There was one girl, Pearl, between me and the next younger brother, Fred, and he was a little too young to milk cows. John was eight years older, and it sorta fell our lot to milk them.

Roy was the next brother older than John, but having somewhat of a handicap, he was not able to milk. So instead, he took care of the horses. His job was to go up into the mow and throw down hay to feed them, clean out the stable, and replace the horses' bedding with clean straw. He was a diligent worker and the stable always looked neat.

In the other end of the barn, there were usually from twelve to fourteen milk cows. Ten down one row of stalls and four down another. All of our cows had names, several of them were named after their previous owners. I'll list the ones I remember: Murry (Murry McCollum), Queen, Bess, Spot, Nancy, Roane, Blackie, Addy (Addy Grice), Canary, and Sam (Sam McCreedy). There was also another area in front of the cattle boarded off to hold veal calves. Out in back of the barn under the corner of the straw stack, we had a bull pen which was usually occupied with a big bruiser.

We had a silo at the end of the cow stable where we kept corn silage for cow feed. The silo was thirty-five feet high, with small openings every couple feet. These openings had wooden doors over them, which had a step built in for climbing up into the silo.

Between the silo and the barn was a small room called the silo room. The silage would fall down the chute into this room to be wheeled in through the stable door in a silage cart. The cart had two main wheels, with a caster wheel on one end, so it would swivel around easily. With the cart piled high with silage, it would be wheeled into the stable through the big door in front of the cows. Each one would be given a big scoop shovelful and topped off with ground feed, such as corn and oats. They liked that feed, and would really produce the milk.

After the cows were all fed, it was time to begin milking. Some of those years we had a milking machine. It was a De Lavalle, gasoline powered milker, and we made the mistake of letting the motor block freeze up one winter night, so we ended up milking by hand for quite a while.

We normally used a one-legged milk stool, and a ten or twelve quart pail. In the corner of the stable in back of the cows, sat two or three ten-gallon milk cans with a strainer in one of them. As we finished milking a cow, we would strain the milk into one of the cans. When the milking was finished, the cans of milk were carried around to the milk house and set into a large, cool water tank. This would protect it from souring until Harry Dyke, our milkman came the next morning to pick it up and then deliver it to the creamery. We would usually save out approximately a gallon for use in the house.

As I mentioned, I didn't especially like this part of the chores. Some of our cows were not too gentle, and occasionally one would kick at me or raise her hind foot up and set it down in the milk pail. I don't mind telling you, that kind of a deal tried me to the limit. John was a little more easygoing.

Another phase of the chores was training the young calves to drink milk from a pail. If you have never tried it, you can't begin to appreciate this nearly as much. Well anyway, after the calves were a few days old, they would be taken from their mother and trained to drink out of a pail. To accomplish this feat, we got a small amount of milk in a ten-quart pail--emphasis on the small (maybe a quart). I'll explain why in a minute. Then we went into the pen where that little mully headed, hungry darling was and got a hammer lock around his neck.

Next, we reached into the pail and got our fingers dripping with warm milk. Then, since he wanted to suck everything in sight anyway, we just let him suck the milk off our fingers. Little by little, as he got accustomed to that, we slowly led his mouth down into the milk. If we were lucky, we may have gotten him to drink after two or three tries.

But, of course, the other thing we had to endure was that those little monkeys just loved to butt their heads into their mother while they were sucking. If we didn't watch, they would also butt the bucket of milk right up into our face. Now do you see what I meant earlier about starting with a small amount of milk?

After just a few days, all we had to do was set the pail down in front of them, and they would devour it in a minute or two. When they were a little older, we would switch them over to skim milk. Skim milk was produced by running the whole milk through a device called a cream separator. We poured the milk into the tank on the top and turned the hand crank. The cream came out one spout, and the skim milk came of out the other.

John and I enjoyed singing while we milked. I guess our whole family liked to sing, so this just came natural for us. As we sat there on our stool milking away, we would sometimes get to singing to the top of our voices. When we would sing fast songs, we always got the milking done sooner. We sang all kinds of songs: gospel songs, Negro spirituals, and popular songs. I want to point out right here that John could sing a pretty mean tenor, so we would harmonize. The fact that he was eighteen and I was ten didn't seem to matter.

One such time in the evening as we were milking along, we must have gotten carried away and were really cutting loose on "Swing Low, Sweet Chariot" or some such song. We both were putting in all the little curly cues, when all of a sudden the stable door opened and there stood John Graham, a friend and neighbor of ours. John and I stopped our grand concert right in mid-air. He said, "Don't stop just because I came in."

Was he kidding? He couldn't have paid us enough to start up again. It was plain to see that he was noticeably tickled, and John and I were noticeably embarrassed.

And as I look back on those scenes, there is somewhat of a longing to return. I guess life seemed to be so much more fun then.

Part Three

1931 - 1937

One

Winter Nightmare

The winter of 1933 I will never forget. In the afternoon of that early December day, the bitter cold north wind howled, sending swirls of dry snow drifting across in front of the barn. John and I started a little early to get the cattle in out of the cold. It seemed like somewhat of a haven in there when the cattle and horses were all inside the barn at the same time. It was surprising how much their body heat warmed up the stable. We were sure thankful that none of them would have to be left outside on a night like this.

In an hour or so it would be time to start the evening chores. Earlier in the afternoon I had taken the scoop shovel and cleared a path through the snow from the cow stable door to the milk house. But you would have never known it, because that strong north wind just kept driving the loose snow down between the toolshed and the silo.

We had an additional problem at the barn that afternoon, and Pa and John were trying to decide what to do about it. The mercury had plummeted way down below zero the night before, and we woke up to frozen water pipes in the mow above the cow stable. We had a large water storage tank up there, that gravity fed water to the automatic drinking cups at each stall. The tank was set up on legs about three feet above the hay mow floor, so as to allow a work space for servicing the pipes, etc.. It was very inconvenient, especially in cold weather, to be without water in the stable. For this reason, Pa and John decided to thaw out the pipes.

It was late in the afternoon but still light enough that we didn't need the lantern in the barn as Roy and I began the chores. He went in on the barn floor and started pitching hay into the horses' mangers, while I wheeled the silage cart into the cow stable and scooped out a heaping shovelful for each cow. I opened the granary door, which was nearby, and from a five-gallon bucket of ground grain, gave each cow about one quart each on top of the silage. Then to be sure they all stayed healthy, I also sprinkled a tablespoonful of Moorman's Mineral (a dark red powder) on top of the ground feed. Boy, did I love the spicy smell of that stuff!

With the feeding done, I came around to the front of the barn with the milk cans and pails. Pa and John were at the entrance of the barn floor, filling up the gasoline blowtorch as I came through the silo room door into the stable. Picking up the one-legged milk stool and the ten-quart pail, I prepared to begin milking. The light roar of the blowtorch overhead could be heard throughout the cow stable. Pa and John had crawled back underneath the water tank where all the frozen pipes were and started heating up the water lines. Little did they realize that what they were about to do would totally disrupt our family's normal pattern of life for several months to come.

Almost before they got started, the cobwebs and chaff which hung down around the pipes caught fire, and in seconds the flames had spread up the side of the tank and into the hay mow. "Fire!" they hollered down to Roy and I. We both dropped what we were doing and grabbed a couple of buckets that were nearby. Hurrying out of the barn door to the milk house, we scooped them full of water and rushed back into the barn. One by one, we scurried up the ladder to where Pa and John were, but it was like trying to put out a forest fire with a squirt gun.

I still don't know how he managed it with his physical handicap, but Roy actually carried a five-gallon bucket of water up the ladder to help put out the fire. In just seconds it was obvious to all of us that we were losing the battle. Roy and I hurried back down, and as Pa and John came rushing out from the little crawl space, Pa hollered, "Get the stock out of the barn!" By that time Roy and I had already begun.

I was turning loose all fourteen milk cows and the few calves we had penned up on the one side of the stable. Roy, who was on the other end, began untying the horses. In what seemed like a very short time, Kenny Hobart and another neighbor came into the horse stable to help him. Smoke filled the drive floor and flames were shooting out of the windows in the end of the hay mow. I had finished getting the cows out the north stable door into the barnyard, so I ran to help Roy and the others with the horses. With darkness all around, I approached the front stable door, and as I did there were sounds of what I thought to be a horse walking toward me, clop, clop, clop. But to my utter amazement, the clippity-clop was not a horse walking, but galloping at full speed as he bolted out the door at only an arm's length away.

By this time the fire was getting so hot in front of the horse's mangers, that the men could not get them to hold still long enough to untie their ropes. Fortunately, some of them finally jerked loose and ran out, but even so, one (my buddy Prince) was so badly burned we had to destroy him.

We had been keeping 150 white Leghorn pullets in an enclosure on the south side of the barn floor. There were also two brood sows with their litters, which had the run of the barnyard around the straw stack. All became trapped and were engulfed in the burning debris.

So much to do and so little time.

There were no fire departments close enough to be of any help, so we just prayed that the wind would not carry the sparks on to the other buildings. Fortunately, we were able to save all of them, plus the silo which was just a few feet away. It being of concrete construction, was not severely harmed, only the doors and the silage chute which were made of wood were destroyed.

But what a nightmare that was. We all just walked around helpless, watching as huge billows of black smoke arose up against a cold starlit sky. It was not only our barn and some precious livestock being destroyed, but a year's worth of hay, straw, and hundreds of bushels of grain going up in smoke. Pa just paced back and forth in the front yard. Several of us stood on guard throughout the night to make sure the sparks didn't ignite the dry wood shingles on the roof of the house.

While all this was going on, our oldest brother, Alvin, and his wife, Iva, were on their way home from their honeymoon at Niagara Falls. Alvin told us later that they were somewhere in the vicinity of Marlette, forty to fifty miles southeast of our place, when they began to see the red glow in the sky. He told Iva that he was suspicious of the location of that fire, because it was about in line with the homeplace. Well, the closer they got the more convinced he was. They pulled into our yard around 10:30 or 11:00 p.m., and he was in such a state of shock he could hardly get out of the car.

When the sun came up the next morning, we had cows, calves, and horses all milling around the barnyard. We had wonderful neighbors, including Uncle Tom Smith, who offered us the use of their buildings to house our stock. Since he was my Pa's brother, it seemed right to accept his offer until we could make other arrangements. That was a little inconvenient having to drive both night and morning, one and a half miles each way hauling feed over, and bringing the milk back home. But we were thankful to have the stock protected during that cold winter season.

The sound of hammer and saw could be heard in the days that followed, as the long toolshed was transformed into suitable housing for all our stock. The bleak smoldering remains of the hundreds of bushels of oats and barley underneath the charred barn timbers was a constant reminder for several weeks of that horrible, unforgettable night.

Shortly thereafter, Pa began making plans to build a new barn. He consulted Uncle Walter Goudie, a carpenter, in the planning and construction of the new building.

The seesaw of the crosscut saws in the early days of 1934 heralded the beginning of the long hours that would be spent in our woods, cutting the oak, elm, and basswood that was to eventually become the new barn. To save having to transport the logs miles away, Pa hired a man with a portable sawmill to come and set up right in the woods. Day after day, the ring of the big circular saw rang out as those huge green logs were being changed into the framing lumber. By doing so, it was only a matter of hauling it a short distance to the building sight, where it was neatly stacked beside the chicken house to cure.

The actual construction began in the spring of that year as the weather began to warm up, making it possible to pour the solid concrete walls, which became a good sturdy foundation. Since strength was a factor in the beams and rafters, elm was used almost exclusively because of its superior strength. It was a beautiful sight to see the new barn taking shape as I would come home from grade school each day.

One phase that did require a lot of work on the inside was getting the cow stalls back as they were before. We kept the same layout of the building, so they were again in the same place. The iron pipes that were formed to make the dividers in the original barn had been all bent out of shape from the intense heat. Because of this, we had to do a lot of reshaping of all those pipes to get them back as they were originally.

Finally, along about the middle of the summer, the new barn was all finished, painted up red with white trim. What a beauty! I don't mind telling you, it was a glorious day when we could finally move all of our stock back into the new barn.

Two

Our Heritage

These were some of the experiences that our family shared together, and I believe that through each of them the Lord was working out His plan in our individual lives.

Probably the one thing that left the greatest impact on my life was Pa's and Ma's devotion to the Lord. From my very earliest recollections, it was a common practice, just following breakfast, for Pa and Ma to have us all come into the large dining room and each take a chair. Pa would get down the family Bible and read a portion of Scripture. Then without any additional comment, we would all kneel down, and all those who knew the Lord would pray. When we finished we would get up and go to our various responsibilities, some to grade school, some to high school, and some to work out on the farm.

I know this experience left its mark on each one of us as children. I really believe that it is impossible to be regularly exposed to God's Word without it making a difference in our lives. Pa and Ma were not much to preach at us, but by their godly example, I know they had a great impact on all of our lives.

They were also regular in church attendance. We all attended the Colwood United Brethren Church. I don't

111

consciously remember any of us rebelling against going to church. I, for one, will admit that much of the time I was more interested in just being with my friends than I was in the Sunday School or sermons.

But at age eleven, during a series of meetings at the church, I came under conviction and realized I had to make a choice; God's way or my way. I remember I had trouble sleeping nights for a while, because I was so disturbed about my sin. I came home from school one day and went to the barn to do the chores. Walking into the cow stable through the silo room door and passing alongside the first cow, I remember either saying out loud or within myself, "All right, I'll go God's way." At that moment a load of guilt was lifted off my shoulders, and I was born again.

There have been ups and downs in my devotion to the Lord, and I have failed in so many ways, but I can truthfully say, He has never failed me. The Lord is so gracious and will always welcome us back home to Himself.

I am thankful for salvation, and also for a Ma and Pa who cared enough about each of us to set a godly example and to pray. The fruit of their lives will be in evidence for many generations to come.

My prayer is that my life will also make an impact for good on all my descendants. I want to testify that our God is faithful and His mercies are new every morning. I want to thank Him personally for sparing my life on numerous occasions as I was growing up on the farm. Praise His name!

Three

Nothing Stays the Same
(A Glimpse into the Future)

Marian and I, with our two children, had moved away from the old home community in 1954. We spent the next twenty-six years in Florida. On one of our return visits to Michigan for the Will and Susanna reunion, we took a drive around the old homeplace. It hardly resembled what I once remembered as home. The orchard was gone--the fences were gone--and some of the buildings were gone. It was a rather sad experience.

However, the sight that effected me more emotionally was what I saw when we drove down the Remington Road past the old grade school where our whole family had attended. The school building had been turned into a private dwelling. But probably the biggest shock of all was to look across the road from it and see a large storage granary on the very spot where a thriving Methodist church used to stand.

I remember as a young boy going with Ma, Pa, and family to special meetings at that church. I can remember one series of meetings in particular. I believe Ray Wilson was the pastor at the time, and he had called in an evangelist by the name of Standridge for those services. I think if I ever saw fire in the pulpit, I saw it in those meetings. There was such an anointing on him that when he gave the invitation for people to come forward to receive Christ, folks came running and crying to the altar. I've been associated with church all my life, but never have I experienced anything quite like that.

Many changes that take place in life are good. But I just wanted to express the sadness that I felt when I saw that huge, galvanized grain silo sitting on the very spot where, at one time, thirsty people knelt down for a drink of the Living Water that Jesus referred to in John 4:14. "But whosoever drinketh of the water that I shall give him shall never thirst; but the water that I shall give him shall be in him a well of water springing up into everlasting life." (KJV)

Four

Flying Low

It was a cold midwinter morning that we woke up to the ground covered with a solid glare of ice and a strong west wind blowing. The four or five of us that were still in grade school had started out walking to school. We got along pretty well until we got down beyond the apple orchard. At that point the wind was so strong, it swept us off into the road ditch. So, we came back to the house and told Pa our predicament, and he got the truck out and took us to school.

About the time we arrived, one of our classmates, Crozier Rutledge who lived a half of a mile west of the school, was gearing up for a memorable trip to school. Let me explain: Crozier had a brand new Elgin Flyer sled, and his plan was to come to school via wind power. So, he set his new sled in the middle of the road on the glare of ice, then gathered up his books and lunch bucket, and got on the sled. He reasoned that if he would hold up the tails of his long overcoat it would act as a sail and get him started--And it did! But what he failed to take into account was how he was going to get stopped once he got to the school.

Well, the sled glided forward smoothly, and quickly began picking up momentum. By then he sure didn't need the sail, so he dropped his coattail and secured his books and lunch bucket. Down the road he came, faster and faster. He gripped the side of the sled with both hands and sailed on, probably 30 mph by now. But how was he going to get the thing stopped when he got there?

Now I want to interject here the choices he had: Stay on the road and probably end up in Cass City, ten miles east, or turn enough to land in the schoolyard. The difficulty with the later choice is that the yard dropped about three feet below the road, and where he would have to turn in was a row of big maple trees, the well pump, and the flagpole. The flagpole was smaller than the trees and a little closer to the road, so in the few seconds he had to make up his mind, he chose the flagpole.

You know, those sleds had a steering bar down in front that you controlled with your feet. So, here he came flying off the road, headed for the pole, and BAAMM! The left end of the steering arm caught the flagpole at around 30 mph. Fortunately, Crozier went off on the right side of the pole, sprawling out into the yard and scattering his books, papers, and lunch bucket high, wide and handsome, all across the schoolyard. Poor guy, he never did recover all of his things.

My brother, Alvin, was living on the Henry McDurmond farm one mile east, and he found some of Crozier's workbooks and papers laying along the fence out in the field the following spring!

Five

Holiday Times

The Christmas season was always special for us kids, even though at times there wasn't much in the way of gifts. Money was pretty scarce during the depression years. One year in particular, if I'm not mistaken, each of us received a penny pencil and a writing tablet. (A penny pencil was a plain one with the eraser set right into the end without the metal sleeve to hold it, costing a penny.)

It didn't seem to matter that the gifts were simple. We had the fun of all being together and doing such things as stringing popcorn for the tree decorations, playing out in the snow, ice skating, etc.. Other special treats were for Mabel and Mary to make fudge, and while they were doing that we would go to the basement and make homemade ice cream in an old crank-type freezer. Many of those winters we had our own ice, stored away in the icehouse underneath a couple feet of sawdust.

You may be wondering where we got the ice to put in the icehouse. When the creeks would freeze over real thick, the men would cut out blocks of ice with a saw, haul them in, and bury them under the sawdust. We would have ice way

117

into the spring for making ice cream and for use in the icebox.

Some of those early years, it was the custom for Grandma and Grandpa Dettweiler to invite our family down for Christmas dinner. Whenever I think about it, I can almost feel the excitement of our whole family climbing into our two cars, a 1927 Buick and a 1929 Model A Ford, and heading for Grandpa's. Before we even got into their house, I would begin to anticipate the smell of dinner cooking. As they opened the front door to greet us, two distinct smells would float through the air; mustard pickles and molasses cookies. As we got inside the house, the smell of chicken cooking and fresh baked bread would begin to blend in with all the other smells.

The dinner would usually consist of the following: fried chicken, mashed potatoes, gravy, homemade noodles, dumplings, homemade bread, pickle relish, gelatin salad, mustard pickles, and fresh apple or cherry pie. Now do you see why I can still remember?!

Six

Tricky Sisters

One Christmas, Roy, John, and I decided to play a trick on the girls. The upstairs in our house was divided into three big bedrooms, plus a large open area at the head of the stairs, which also was used at times as a bedroom. I believe all the girls were still at home, and they occupied the two bedrooms on the west end of the house. Our plan was to barricade and tie their doors shut after they had gone to bed on Christmas Eve, so they couldn't beat us downstairs on Christmas morning.

We waited until everything quieted down in their end of the house. Then we gingerly carried our clothesline rope and all the other gear up there and proceeded to secure both their bedroom doors. In no time we had that area looking like Fort Knox. All feeling great about our accomplishment, we tip-toed around through the hallway and into our rooms, turning in for the night. We were soon off into sugarplum land, and in no time at all, it was Christmas morning.

But something had gone wrong. Somehow or other, we must have underestimated the cleverness of those gals, because as we tip-toed out into the hallway on our way downstairs, there was our "girl-proof" barricade, ropes, etc., all in disarray, and those clever gals were already down around the Christmas tree! Needless to say, we never tried that trick again.

Seven

Family Times

(A Flashback)

Pa had owned a Model T Ford when I first knew about cars. Later on he bought the Buick, and I'll never forget that car. It was very comfortable and roomy to ride in. Many times on nice summer Sunday afternoons, Pa and Ma would load all of us younger ones (Rosella, Ruth, Pearl, probably Fred was the baby, and I) into the Buick and leisurely ride back to the woods, which was at the far end of our farm. One of Pa's favorite songs which we would all join in on was "Keep on the Sunny Side of Life." I'll see if I can remember the words.

"Keep on the sunny side,
always on the sunny side.
Keep on the sunny side of life.
It will help you day by day,
it will drive the gloom away,
if you keep on the sunny side of life."

Sometimes we would spend an hour or so back there just enjoying the beauty of the woods. As the warm rains of spring would begin to soak into the ground, lots of little wild flowers began to push up through the leaves: violets, jack-in-the-pulpits, and lady slippers were some of the favorites. I believe it was little outings such as these that helped to keep our family knit together so closely.

It was in 1929 that Pa bought the brand new Model A Ford Town Sedan. Special features of this model were: two shiny, chrome-plated curb lights mounted just ahead of the windshield on each side, and a manifold hot air heater with heat ducts running to the front and rear seats connected to little heat registers on the floor.

This was the first car we had with a gas gauge that could be read without getting out of the car. The tank was just ahead of the dash, and the gauge was in a little oval-shaped window in the middle of it. Some cars had a gauge on the top of the tank, but it could not be seen while sitting in the car. A person had to get out of the car to check the gas. Others didn't have a gauge at all, which meant you would have to take a stick, such as a twelve-inch ruler, and dip it in the tank.

One of the first long trips I remember taking in our new Ford was to Ann Arbor to visit our brother, Roy, who had undergone a serious operation. While he was a baby his head was injured when Ma fell down the stairs with him. Later on he began to have seizures. At age fifteen they took him to Ann Arbor University Hospital for surgery on his head. It was a very serious, but successful operation. I was just one of five or six of us that went that day to see him.

I was fascinated by new cars. I believe it was 1933 or '34 that Henry Ford came out with the first V 8. Elden had purchased one of those early models. One day, Pa borrowed it to make a trip to Unionville, which was about fourteen miles away. He wasn't accustomed to driving such a spiffy, smooth running car, and admitted to us later that he had

121

driven almost all the way there with the car still in second gear. V 8's became very popular because of their smoothness.

Eight

Under the Pile

It was always exciting to have company come to our house, especially relatives. This would give all of us kids an occasion to lay down the hoe and pitchfork and just enjoy life for awhile. During the summer of 1936, we had a pleasant surprise. Uncle Elden Dettweiler's family came from California to visit for the first time in twenty-one years!

They were staying at Grandma and Grandpa Dettweiler's home near Caro. Ma and Pa invited them to spend one whole day with us. Their family consisted of Uncle Elden, Aunt Beatrice, Arthur, Beulah, Eloise, and baby Mertice.

Eloise was about two or three years old and not accustomed to rough and tumble farm life. Pearl and I wanted to show her a good time, so I suggested that we give her a ride on Ol' Tony.

Tony was one of those good-natured old horses, about twenty years old, that wouldn't hurt a soul. He was easygoing enough, and I didn't think he even needed a bridle. It so happened that he was already outside in the barnyard on the north end where the cow stable was. I decided that we could all get on him and just let him carry us around and around the barnyard. We nudged him over to the rail fence where all three of us could climb on. I helped them up, and then jumped on in front of them.

Pearl was holding Eloise on her lap, with me in front, and away we went at a nice steady gait. We had made a few big circles around the yard when all of a sudden, Tony spotted a little crack in the cow stable door. It was the type of a door that rolls on a track and just happened to be open about a foot. That was enough to attract ol' Tony, so he swung around and with a determined gait headed for it.

As we approached the door, I had visions of us all getting our knees scrubbed up as we squeezed through that small opening. So I took drastic measures and stuck both my feet right straight out in front of me as we headed for the stable. Yep, you guessed it. As Tony (pictured below) plowed through the stable door, it wiped all three of us, slick and clean off his back and down into the mud. Pearl hit the ground first holding Eloise, and then I landed on top of them. I can't imagine why Pearl got so upset with me. Maybe that's what you call being under the circumstances.

Nine

Eerie Sounds of Night

A highlight of the summer months was the Tuscola County Fair at Caro. One of the most vivid memories of those times was when I would have been in my early teens. Pa offered to take us younger kids to the fair. I don't know whether Pearl went or not, but the three younger boys (Fred, Dick and Don) and I went. We left right after lunch and got to the fairgrounds around one o'clock. When Pa let us out at the gate after buying our tickets, he said to us, "I want you all back at the car about 4:30 p.m. so we can get home in time to do the chores."

We all said, "O.K."

Well, as you all know time seems to get away from you when you are having fun. The younger boys took off together one way and I went by myself to see all the sights.

About halfway through the afternoon, I ran across Leslie Peasley. He was one of Uncle Tom Smith's hired men and about my age. Les was the type of fellow that seemed to always have a girlfriend hanging on his arm. Well, today was no exception. The only problem was, he was getting tired of this one and asked me if I would like to take her off his hands.

I said, "Sure, why not." I had never had a girl dumped onto me before, so I didn't really know how to conduct myself.

They had one attraction called a Tilt-a-Whirl, and I asked her if she would like to take a ride. She said she would, so we rode that one for a while. We spent the rest of the afternoon just strolling around through the midway.

Pa had said to be back to the car by 4:30, and when he said 4:30, he didn't mean give or take 30 minutes. I glanced at my watch, and with dismay exclaimed, "Oh, no! It can't be 4:20!" Prying her fingers loose from my arm, I bade her adieu, and skedaddled. I beat it out to the car, or I should say out to where the car had been. Yup, you guessed it. Pa had already taken the younger ones and high-tailed it for home. (I found out later that my watch was not reading correctly. Instead of being 4:20 when I looked, it was already past 4:30.)

Now was I ever in trouble! I not only had to find a ride home, but what would happen after I get there? (I should mention that it was seven or eight miles back to the house.) Then my frantic search of the fairgrounds began as I looked for someone I knew who just might be going out toward Colwood. I finally spotted Vern Cross with his son, Alvin. I explained to them my predicament, and Vern half-heartedly said, "I guess you can ride out with us." The only problem was, they had another hour or so of sight-seeing to do. I couldn't imagine waiting later into the night before we would even leave, yet I had no choice. It was either that or walk, and I didn't relish either prospect.

Finally, here they came trudging wearily out toward the entrance where I was anxiously waiting. By now it was already pitchdark. With dread, I climbed into their 1929 Model A Ford, and we started for home. They lived about one mile west of the Remington School, and our home was one-half mile east and one-half mile north of the school. I thought that Vern would take me right over to our place, but I

126

guess he thought that was too much trouble. Instead, he dropped me off at the school corner around 10 p.m.

I had walked that route many times to and from school in the daylight--but never after dark--alone. I don't mind telling you, I was scared and was hearing all sorts of crazy noises. Probably no one knows what the record was for that mile, but I'm sure I broke all the previous ones. When I finally arrived at the house, I had mixed emotions. Relief, of course, because I was safe--uneasy, because I wasn't sure what Pa would say or do.

You're probably all wondering what Pa did say the next morning, but I think he must have figured my having to find a way home was punishment enough. But I did apologize for not being at the car in time to go home with them.

Ten

Hazards of Growing Up

As I got a little older, my three younger brothers, Fred, Dick, and Don were coming along, and the older ones were leaving home. So things began to change.   Instead of me being the youngest of the work force, I became the oldest. Just as it had been for all the older boys, the younger ones fell right into the routine of chores, morning and night, as well as all the other duties around the farm.

By this time we did have more conveniences, such as electricity in all the farm buildings.   In the mid-thirties Pa bought our first John Deere combine, which meant far less work at threshing time.   Instead of it taking weeks to harvest our grain, we could wait until it was dead-ripe, and then go right into the field, cutting and threshing all in one operation.

As I look back on it now, I believe I might have taken my younger brothers for granted.   A large portion of the work began to fall on their shoulders, as I became much more involved with Pa in outside activities. But more on that later.

First, I want to share a few of our escapades as four energetic boys. One of the things we enjoyed doing when the three little "scoopen-dykes" were still quite young was for me to lay down on my back on the ground and pull my knees up to my chin with my feet in the air. I would have one of them sit on my feet facing away from me, then with a burst of energy I would send them sailing through the air, hopefully landing right side up. It didn't always work out that way. By the way, it is only by the grace of God that we are still here to talk about it!

I remember another occasion the four of us had some idle time on our hands and were goofing around in the horse stable. I can still picture the exact spot. There was a considerable amount of straw on the floor in back of the horses, so I was going to try another of my neat tricks. This time Fred was the victim.

The deal was for him to face toward me, then bend his head down just above my knees. At this point, I would bend forward over him, and put my arms around under his backside. When he was ready, I would rare up, and flip him completely over and back onto his feet. Or at least that's what was supposed to happen.

But even some of the best laid plans get derailed. And this time something did go drastically wrong. I don't know whether I underestimated his weight or what, but rather than making a full revolution, he only made a half. Instead of landing on his feet as planned, he landed on his head. Clunk! I don't mind telling you, I was afraid he had broken his neck. For some unknown reason, Fred seemed to be anxious to change games!

As I look back on those days, it seems that Fred and I were in quite a few little scrapes together. Maybe it was because he was the brother nearest me in age. One Saturday afternoon when we didn't have anything in particular to do, Fred and I decided to have some fun. Our plan was to take a little ride on the doodle-bug. We usually kept it in a long narrow lean-to shed between the workshop and the toolshed, with just barely room to squeeze it in. It didn't have a starter, which meant one of us had to crank it. I decided to do it since I was the oldest. Fred climbed up on the seat, which was also the gas tank, and he worked the choke button while I cranked. I need to point out that it was extremely important to see that the doodle-bug was out of gear before you started cranking.

Well, sure enough it was in gear, and it did start--on the first crank over. Here it came, crowding me into the end of the building. It was only the quick thinking on Fred's part that kept me from being pinned to the wall. He jammed it into reverse, and it started backing out of the shed. Hallelujah! Whoops! Oh no, here he comes again. All of a sudden, Fred realized that we didn't want the folks to know we were playing with the doodle-bug. He shifted back into a forward speed, and here he came at me again! By this time, he had presence of mind enough to shift into reverse again, and when he did, I real quick-like jumped up onto the seat and turned the key off. You can't tell me that we don't have angels watching out for us. I think the ones assigned to my case got in a considerable amount of overtime!

Eleven

Mossbacks

The afternoon was balmy with a light breeze blowing the yellow oat chaff around in front of the barn where the big threshing machine had been sitting for the past two days. Four or five pigeons mingled in among a couple of dozen white Leghorns as they scratched for the leftover kernels of grain at the entrance to the barn floor.

Fred, Dick, Don, and I were tossing the softball around at the west end of the garage as Pa pulled up into the yard with the little Model H John Deere. In just a few minutes we would be off to the barn and back to the usual routine. After Pa got the tractor backed into the long toolshed, he came out and said, "Ma and I are planning to go to the conference tomorrow in Carson City. I guess you mossbacks can take care of things here, can't you?"

"We'll do our best," I answered, pleased that he was willing to entrust the care of the farm into the hands of us younger guys. (Mossback was a name that Pa frequently used to refer to us who were younger. We weren't offended by it, because we knew that it was often used during those years in referring to someone younger who you cared about. Actually, we were pleased to be recognized that way.)

From left to right: Fred, Dick, and Don

Where they were going was to the annual United Brethren Church Conference in Carson City. Pa went on into the house, and we ceased our little fun time and headed for the barn to do our usual chore detail. Don, being the youngest, took care of the chickens and gathered the eggs. He was a little feller that didn't take his jobs too seriously--or so I, his big brother thought. In other words, it seemed that he didn't think it necessary to get all nerved up about the work involved. Being the oldest of the four, I guess I really got on his case a lot. He actually did do his work exceptionally well for being only seven or eight years old.

Fred, Dick, and I sorta worked at barn chores together: feeding and watering, making sure the horses and cattle had clean straw under them for bedding, as well as milking the fourteen cows. The north end of the barn was the cow stable, and one of us would climb up into the silo and throw down enough silage for night and morning. As soon as the cows were fed, all three of us got a milk pail and a stool, and in

132

about 45 minutes were all finished milking. Two of us carried the ten-gallon milk cans out into the cool water tank, while the other one took a fork and distributed clean straw around under each of the cows. He also made sure the veal calves in the pen at the back of the stable had water in their trough. Chores all done, I flipped off the lights, and we were free until a little before daybreak the next morning.

In the morning, as soon as breakfast was over, Pa and Ma loaded their luggage into the 1935 Buick and were off to the conference. Now there we were, us four mossbacks, as well as Ruthie and Pearl. I think Pa must have forgotten how hazardous it can be with the likes of us four in charge of things on a big farm. Who knows, maybe he knew something we didn't know. Well, anyway, here we were with quite a bit of free time to put to good use. And desiring to be good stewards and not wanting to waste any of it, I started racking my brain trying to come up with some fun things to do.

For a starter, we decided to spend Sunday afternoon playing over at the McDurmond barn. Alvin and Iva lived there at the time, but they had also gone to the conference. When we got home from Sunday School and church, we eagerly waited for lunch to be over. After getting into some play clothes, we hiked over to Alvin's with great anticipation, knowing that there were some long hay ropes to play on in the barn.

Unfortunately, the three younger ones usually trusted my judgment about the things we tried. Well, I devised this little plan. There was a rope that went all the way from the floor to the peak of the barn, then through a pulley and back down to the hay mow. The scheme was for Fred (bless his heart) to take one end of the rope, climb up, and sit on one of the crossbeams near the eaves. I would take the other end of the rope and climb all the way up to the peak and jump off.

I had figured that, with my extra weight, it would create enough momentum to carry Fred all the way across the barn. Well, it certainly did that--and much more! In fact, it not only did what I anticipated, but it did it in about half the time. There we were, Fred gripping his end of the rope on the first level, and me gripping my end way up there in the peak. I said, "Here goes," as I leaped out into space. Poor Fred blasted off that beam, sailed through the air all the way to the other side of the barn, crashed into the roof, and then bounced back down to the hay mow below. Wow! I'm not sure, but I believe he set a record for flying inside an old hay barn. I can't imagine why Dick and Don didn't want the same ride. Can you?

We can laugh about it now, but it really wasn't funny. If my memory serves me correctly, we all decided to calm down a little before someone got hurt worse. We had plenty of fun anyway just swinging on the ropes back and forth over the barn floor.

Twelve

The Flea Swatter

My teachers in grade school were Mr. Edgar Hodges, beginner - third grade; Mrs. Maude Blades, fourth - fifth; Ida Thane (who later became my sister-in-law, Ida Smith) sixth - eighth. I got along well in school for the first five or six grades. I was a little younger than some of my friends who were also in my class: Bob Grice, Irene Orban, and a few others.

As we were getting down near the end of the sixth grade year, some of my friends began talking of trying to take the seventh and eighth grades together. They asked Miss Thane if she thought it would be all right, and she agreed. Not wanting to be left behind an extra year, I decided to ask her if I could take the last two years together also. She reluctantly said I could, but I think she questioned whether I should or not. I did take the two grades together, but it turned out to be pretty difficult for me. After graduating from grade school in 1935, I was glad for summer vacation!

High school became very burdensome for me, partially because of the demanding work schedule on the farm. In order to adequately care for all the livestock: milk cows, horses, hogs, and chickens, it took at least a couple of hours, both morning and evening. Then, by squeezing in enough time for breakfast and supper, we young guys found ourselves pretty much on a treadmill. School was about a nine month commitment. I guess I somewhat envied many of my friends who were able to go out for sports or stay after school for band practice, etc..

However, I did enjoy physical education, especially basketball and boxing. The coach at that time (Carl Bowman) seemed to love boxing also. When he realized how much fun some of us seemed to get out of it, he decided to set up an exhibition bout for the high school assembly. I have to confess, I had mixed emotions about a public performance where there was only a 50 - 50 chance of coming out a winner. I probably weighed in at around 160 which, according to the coach, put me in the welter weight class. My opponent for this match was going to be Louis (Flea) Carpenter. (I didn't know it then, but he was also to become somewhat of a relative of the Smith family. His older brother, Bill, married our first cousin, Margurite Smith.)

He was a neat guy to have as a friend and was a very clean boxer. He was about an inch shorter than me but was as hard as nails. I can tell you that although I enjoyed the sport, my confidence level was not all that high, as the scheduled bout drew near. Well, the day for the big event finally arrived. There was also a heavyweight match that same day between Fritz Sealand and Deon Mank.

Flea and I were the first to be called up. We donned our gloves and climbed into the ring. At the sound of the bell, we both came out swinging. His strategy focused on guarding --he was an expert at that. Being a little taller, I seemed to have a slight advantage in my reach, so I capitalized by sending left jabs to the head whenever possible. The bleachers were packed with screaming spectators. "Go get 'em, tiger!" they yelled. What an exciting time that was.

Oh, I know, you're all wondering who won that match. If I remember correctly, they had to come in and separate us before Flea got hurt. *(A-hem!)*

Thirteen

High School On the Lighter Side

The one subject I enjoyed the most was farm crops with Russell Hill as my teacher. I especially enjoyed experimenting with seeds, etc.. Another fun activity was getting ready for the fair. I was a member of the F.F.A. (Future Farmers of America) and each year the organization would sponsor an exhibition. Any of the kids that wanted to could compete in the various contests: livestock, seeds, and so on. My specialty was what we called "grass seed," which included sweet clover, alfalfa, and June clover. I was fortunate enough to win first place several different years, especially with alfalfa and sweet clover. I still have some of my blue ribbons in a desk drawer.

Probably the most fun was getting the seed ready for the show. The school furnished a nice new Clipper Fanning Mill for us to use and it was in the hallway just outside the Ag-room. We would go in there after school or at lunch time and make use of it. Ferris Graham was a friend of mine, who also had seed to get ready, and we worked together taking turns cranking the fanning mill.

For those who may not know what a fanning mill is, let me explain. It was a hand-driven piece of equipment used for cleaning all types of seed. It was approximately 3 feet wide,

4 feet long, and 4 1/2 feet high, with a hopper on top where you poured the seed in. As soon as the crank is turned, the grain begins to sift down onto a shaker that has a screen the proper size for that type of seed. The good seed falls through the screen and ends up in a bin below, while pods or straw, are carried off the end of the screen. There is a fan turning inside, blowing air through the machine to force out the light chaff and other undesirable waste.

Although high school in general was not especially exciting for me, I did enjoy the ride to and from school. There were no buses running out in our neck-of-the-woods, so our transportation was the family car. Our older sister, Mary, was working at the Tuscola County Courthouse, so we rode into town with her that first year. Although her work schedule did not exactly correspond with our school hours, it didn't seem to create a hardship for any of us. I believe we got out of school at 4 p.m. and Mary was off work at 5 p.m. I don't remember how Rosella and Ruthie spent that free hour, but I know what I did--I tried to have fun as usual.

Our cousin, Merrill Goudie, was also in my class and was never in a hurry to go home. He just lived about one and a half miles from town and usually walked to and from school. Between us, we could always conjure up something to get into to take up the slack time. His mom, Aunt Magdalena, ordinarily saw to it that he had at least a couple of dollars with him whenever he left home. I know for many high schoolers today that would be nothing special, but in 1935 it was a whole different ball game. Not every school kid had a pocketful of change.

Merrill, being the good-hearted guy that he was, would often invite me to go with him down to Hooper's Drug Store. I can still remember that very first time climbing up onto the bar stool and each of us ordering a big strawberry soda.

Can't you almost hear that stream of soda water under pressure, causing that fluffy, pink foam to rise up into those tall soda glasses. Wow--what a treat that was after a grueling eight hours of school!

On other days when we weren't sippin' sodas, we spent our time goofing around at the courthouse, waiting for Mary to get off work. The courthouse had very recently been built and was quite an attraction for these two country bumpkins. The marble floors just glistened. Every now and then, I guess we did get a little rowdy, enough to get the attention of the custodian. He would kindly tell us to either quiet down or get out of the building. How can you keep two 13 or 14 year olds quiet?

I'll have to say that, without some of those kinds of experiences, high school would have been extremely boring to this kid. Besides that, look at all those things I might not have learned if I'd gone right straight home after school!

It was nice having Mary driving us to and from school. We never had to worry about our safety when she was at the wheel.

Whoops! I guess I'll have to take that all back. I did worry one time. It was a day during the winter of '35. It had snowed the day before, and some of the snow still lingered and was getting packed in certain places. We were on our way home one afternoon, Mary and Rosella in the front seat, with Ruthie and I in the back of the old Pontiac.

Everything seemed to be going along fine until we got all the way out opposite the cedar swamp across from Wes Lockwood's on the Colwood Road. There seemed to be a long stretch of packed snow that had turned to ice. I was just riding along "scootched" down in my corner of the back seat without a care in the world. The next thing I knew, the back end of the car seemed to move sideways, and at 45 mph or 50 mph that's not funny!

I thought, *what's going on here? I believe we are going into a spin.* Sure enough, before Mary could gain control, we had swapped ends a couple of times. Fortunately, we weren't meeting any other cars, and if I remember correctly, we didn't even slide into the ditch. That did create a little adrenaline rush there for a few seconds, kinda of like being on one of those scary rides at the county fair!

This was just one more case of our Father watching over His kids.

In my sophomore year I had started driving, and by then Pa had traded for a 1935 Buick. The following year John bought an old '21 Buick touring car for the outrageous price of $25.00. He let us use it for our school bus. A touring car was a car with a canvas top and side curtains that had flexible glass for windows. It was really a four-door convertible.

For any of you who are familiar with car tires, these were 21 x 4. With those high, narrow wheels, could that car plow through the snow! The only little problem driving in snow was that it seeped in around the side curtains and accumulated on our laps as we drove along. When we got to our destination, everyone would have to shake the snow out of their clothes as they got out of the car. It was never warm enough to soften the snow, so it would shake off quite easily.

For most of those high school years, our crew consisted of my two sisters, Rosella and Ruthie, as well as Winnifred Terwilligar, Maxine Remington, Ferris Graham, and me. Sometimes on the icy hills over on the lower end of the Remington road, the kids would all have to get out and push to get us up the next hill.

One other little point of interest about one of these trips, which up until now has been kept pretty much a secret. It seems that there was another car load of kids that traveled the same road, but had a few miles farther to come. The driver was Dale Abky. Our last stretch of road was about three miles on M 81 east of Caro (gravel at that time).

One morning as we both happened to merge out onto that road about the same time, I had an idea. "Why not challenge Dale to a race?" So, I looked over and motioned to him, he nodded in agreement, and off we went, gravel stones flying. Dale was driving a 1928 Chevy, we had the 1921 Buick touring car.

It was a terribly silly thing to do. But here we went, side by side on a two-lane gravel road. His Chevy was pretty good at getting up speed, but after we got rolling along on the straight-away, my old quivering and quaking Buick began to pull out ahead. I suppose we were traveling at the unbelievable speed of around 65 mph when we hit the Caro City limits. That's when I decided to call off the race before we caught the attention of the Caro policeman, Clayton Montie. Not wanting to get in trouble with the law, I let up on the gas and fell back single file as we innocently eased down main street. I guess we all did a lot of goofy things back when we were young. By the way, Clayton was one of the most mild-mannered policeman I have ever known.

During my junior year of high school, my Pa began to have quite a bit of trouble with his heart. To make it a little easier for him, I offered to drop out of school to help with the farm work. He really didn't want me to do that, but finally agreed. I was sixteen at the time and had already been involved in just about everything there was to do on the farm, so I just took over most of the work load for him.

The following year I did take a correspondence course in farm management from the LaSalle Extension Institute in Chicago. The Ford Motor Company sponsored this training for a select number of farm boys. I was chosen through a recommendation from Henderson Graham, who had just finished the program. It was the policy of the company to have its graduates recommend other worthy participants.

One of the requirements for being in this program was that I operate a Ford tractor for a given number of hours that summer. We didn't own one, but Bob Milner, a neighbor of ours, let me borrow his Ford tractor for a period of time. I really appreciated the use of it, and it also gave me a very high regard for those little tractors.

Having experienced so many years on the farm, it made the course seem somewhat of a breeze. Even to this day, I have my diploma showing that I did pass.

Fourteen

Fond Memories

(A Flashback)

I'd also like to share a few fond memories I have of my Ma. She was quite a gentle and fun-loving person. Looking back on it now, it seemed that much of her time was spent caring for us little guys. Either she was rocking one of us to sleep while singing or whistling some of the old favorite hymns, or she was moving about the kitchen preparing delicious meals.

I can still see her standing at the kitchen counter, with streaks of silver beginning to blend in with her beautiful, dark wavy hair. And with what appeared to be the energy of a twenty year old, she would roll that big ball of bread dough back and forth on the bread board, then pause a moment and dust the flour off her hands.

Many are the times as we kids would come home from school or in from work, we would find a nice row of freshly baked loaves of bread with the crust still glistening from a coat of real dairy butter. And since it wouldn't have been showing our appreciation by just letting them sit there undisturbed, we would go to the silverware drawer, pull out the long bread knife, and cut off the end piece about one inch thick. WOW! Next, we laid it on a plate, spread a thick layer of brown sugar over it, then went to the ice-box and got the pitcher of fresh cream to pour over the sugar. I can almost taste it now. That was a real treat for boys who were hungry most of the time.

She cared a lot about each one of us kids. In my mind's eye I can see her now as she left what she was doing to come and wipe away the tears with the corner of her long blue and white gingham apron smudged with flour. That kind of caring sure did help to heal the hurts and bruises.

Ma liked poetry, and she would recite it to us as she held us in her lap. I'll see if I can put down a couple of them.

"O robin, robin red-breast,
O robin, robin dear,
The robin sings so sweetly
in the falling of the year."

* * * *

"Early to bed, and early to rise,
Makes a man healthy, wealthy, and wise."

There were many others that slip my mind now, but I just want to say that the time she spent with us as we were growing up has left a lasting impression for good.

Just a few other little happenings during my early years, which had mostly to do with Pa. It got to be a custom at our house on birthdays to do something that would be remembered, especially on the boy's birthdays.

Of course, every one knows that you are supposed to receive a whippin' on your birthday. To stay with tradition, Pa would usually wait until after the evening meal that day before he took action. While we were still sitting around the long table, he would rise from his chair and come around to the one who had just turned a year older that day, drag them out of their chair, and then go at it. When I say "go at it," I mean just that. He always gave us the right to resist, but he usually stuck to it until we were both rolling around under the table, turning over chairs or whatever, until he got in the last "One to grow on." It was all in fun, and I would say that seldom was any of us offended at the treatment we received.

Pa spent a lot of time playing with us. He liked playing baseball as well as we did. Almost every Sunday afternoon in the summertime we would play ball. We had a nice area right at the west end of the garage that served as the ball diamond.

Those who were acquainted with Pa knew how spry he was. I can still remember many times as he would come home from maybe selling a load of grain or possibly a piece of farm equipment. He would jump out of his car, come in the house with his straw hat in his hand, and begin dancing a little jig around the room. During this little performance, he would say,

"Sold again and got the tin,
And got a can to put it in."

Whenever he would go though this little routine, we all knew that things had gone well for him that day.

Pa also loved to sing. I can almost hear him singing at the top of his voice even yet such songs as the "Old Rugged Cross" or "An Unclouded Day" as he drove the old John Deere tractor back and forth across the field.

Fifteen

Over She Goes

I must have been around fourteen along about the latter part of May, 1936, as the navy beans were around two or three inches high. Pa decided to do some cultivating with the little John Deere tractor. He was all ready to head to the bean field in back of our barn, when he asked me to take the Model "D" tractor over to the McDurmond farm and bring home the field cultivator. This was just one of the pieces of equipment that we used on each of the farms we rented. Alvin and Iva were living there at the time. This farm was 1/2 mile south and 1/2 mile east of our place. On the right side of the road going east was a very deep ditch. The big tractor was getting a little loose in the steering gear and was inclined to wander.

I had gone the first half-mile and was heading east, cruising right along in high gear. I was also watching our neighbor, Jack Donahue, who happened to be running his tractor in a field nearby. You know, I had just taken my eyes off the road for an instant, but it was long enough for the tractor to wander to the right. As it did, the front wheel dropped off the shoulder of the road.

The ditch bank was steep and about eight feet deep. I knew I had to act quickly, but reasoned that if I tried to pull it back onto the road, it would probably flip over. But before I could do anything, the tractor did flip completely upside down in the bottom of the ditch.

Fortunately, I had been standing up straddle the seat when I realized that it was going over. In a flash, I hurled my body backward and found myself diving head first into the bottom of the road ditch, a distance of at least ten feet. I landed on my head and shoulders just behind where the tractor seat plunged deeply into the mud!

John Deere Model "D"

Thankful that I wasn't under the tractor, my next thought was, *This thing could explode any minute with all that fuel in the tank!* But, fortunately, the motor just rumbled to a stop as I went scrambling up the ditch bank.

Jack Donahue told me later, "I didn't know what happened to you, Bill. I saw you going down the road, and all of a sudden you vanished." The ditch was so deep he couldn't even see the tractor turned over in it.

Well, I was a little bruised up, shook up, and scared, because I didn't know what Pa's reaction would be. I walked back home with fear and trembling, and instead of going to the house to tell Ma, I went straight to the bean field where Pa was cultivating. He sure was surprised to see me back home so soon. When I told him what had happened, he made no comment at all. I could hardly believe it. All he said was, "Why don't you take my place here, and I'll go see about it."

He walked up to the house and got Ma, and on their way out the door, he matter-of-factly mentioned, "Bill tipped the big tractor over." That was all he said.

At first, Ma was so struck with fear she couldn't speak. They both got into the car and started out of the driveway. By then, Ma had held back the anxiety about as long as she could and asked, "Where's Bill?"

Pa's response was, "Don't worry, he's okay. I just had him take my place cultivating, so I could go and check out the damage to the big tractor."

When Pa came home from surveying the damage, he went directly down to our neighbor, Roy Vader, and got him to come with his big W-30 McCormick-Deering tractor to pull ours over and back up onto the road. It so happened that the bottom of the ditch was soft enough that there was not a great deal of damage to the tractor. It did break off the two stacks, exhaust pipe, and air cleaner, and bent the fenders, the steering wheel, and shaft. We were able to get it repaired and were thankful for the Lord's protection. My only injuries were a stiff neck and some bruises on the back of my legs where I tried to jump free from the sharp edges of the metal seat.

It was along about this time that Pa became involved in various activities outside the farm. For a few years he was the field manager for the Clarke Canning Company in Caro. Later on he joined with two other successful farmers in forming a corporation known as The Caro Sugar Beet Growers Association. Otto Montie was president, Emory Lounsbury was secretary, and Pa was treasurer. He always took his work very seriously. Keeping those books was an extra burden for him, and I tried as best I could to help him in the evenings after the chores were done.

Through this company they bought and sold fertilizer to the farmers in the surrounding area. Pa also agreed to be responsible for distributing the fertilizer to the various farms. I happened to be the oldest boy home at this time, which gave me firsthand experience handling 125 pounds bags of fertilizer.

They would order it by the train carload, and we would take our truck down to Caro to load it out of the freight cars. We delivered it to the farms where we usually would have to carry it into their barns or other storage areas. Rummaging through some of my old papers, I ran across a journal dated 1939. In one of its entries dated April 25, I noted that Pa and I delivered 218 bags of fertilizer to six different locations. I don't mind telling you, that was work! Whenever I think about it, I can't help but wonder if the extra work and responsibility of that business might have helped to shorten Pa's life.

September
1939   October

Sat 30   I took a load of our beans to the elevator
at Collins ($ 2.75 per 100) Pa & Harold fixed the
corn fodder. In the afternoon Pa & I took
the truck to Striffler garage. We left the
truck there to get the clutch put in. We
drove the Buick over to Fairgrove to look
at a beet loader. Harold & Alvin worked
over in the McDurmon barn cleaning
up the beans off from the barn floor.

Sun 1   Pa, Ma, Mary and Clifford went out to North
Star to Paul & Rosellas.

Mon 2   Harold & Roy, I loaded up 2 loads of corn
in the 6 acre field. Pa went to see about
getting the truck at the garage. Roy & Harold
dug a few potatoes. Alvin, Pa, & I tried
out the beet lifter. Afternoon Alvin, Harold,
I took the truck over to Carls to thresh
beans.

Tue 3   Pa & I started cutting corn in the up acres.
Roy & Harold took the car & trailer & brought
Roys sow home here. Harold & Carl Smith
took a truck load of Carls beans to Collins.
Afternoon Whitfield brought the seed &
fodder oil here. Harold helped Uncle Tom
thresh beans. Roy to grain binder, & got
Roys to cut soybeans. Alvin & Pa put up the fodder

Sixteen

A Run For Cover

As I look back now I realize how close I stayed to my Pa the first five or six years of my life, then again the last three of four year of his life. Let me share an experience that Pa and I had when I was sixteen.

He and I had gone with the truck down north of Colwood to the fifty-acre farm we had rented. There was a long drainage ditch that ran almost the full length of the farm lined on both sides with trees. Pa wanted to get rid of them and level the ditch in order to farm the entire area. I'm not sure he realized how much hard work would be involved. There were a couple incidents connected with that job that were kinda scary.

We had taken our big John Deere tractor down there to be used for pulling some of the smaller trees. I was operating the tractor, and Pa had attached the long chain to a pretty good size tree about six feet above the ground. I need to explain here that this particular tractor had a hand operated clutch. Instead of a pedal, it was a long arm that stood straight up on the right side of the steering wheel. To engage the clutch, it had to be pushed forward.

There we were all ready to pull the tree over, but I had underestimated its size and height. When the tractor lunged forward, the big bushy top did also. Over it came, crashing down onto the tractor, flattening me right down between the fender and the steering wheel. If that wasn't enough, the heavy branches had also jammed the clutch lever forward so I couldn't stop the tractor!

After being pinned down there for a few seconds, the big drive-wheels spinning as they chewed up the sod, I did have presence of mind enough to reach through and pull the throttle lever back, causing the tractor to stall. Boy, was I shook up and scared. Finally, I was able with a little finagling to dig my way out of the jungle of tree limbs.

The next day we went back over there again, but this time we decided to get rid of some of the tree stumps with dynamite. Since we felt that it was important to get the charge of dynamite as far under the stump as possible, we spent an hour or so digging out around the roots of one of them with shovels and a grub hoe. With that done, Pa walked over to the chest on the back of the truck and brought back a couple of sticks of dynamite. Tying them together and attaching the fuse, he slipped them down underneath the stump. Then to help hold the force of the blast directly under the stump, we scooped much of the loose dirt back in around the roots again.

With everything all ready, Pa had me move the truck a good distance away, because you never knew where the stump would come down. So I drove it out about 150 yards, while Pa got ready to light the fuse. When he was ready to strike the match, he said, "As soon as I light this fuse, we better hightail it to the truck!" He didn't have to tell me more than once. The instant he said "Go," we beat it across the field and jumped into the truck cab.

As we waited in the stillness of the truck, peering out the back window, I began thinking, *What if that dude doesn't go off?* Then all of a sudden, BOOM! Away went a huge section of the stump, hurling its way up into the air, tumbling end over end. Where do you suppose it landed? You guessed it. About fifty feet to one side of the truck. After this episode, I believe Pa became a little discouraged with the whole deal and decided it wasn't worth all the hassle. So we gathered up our tools and headed back home. As far as I know the tree-lined ditch still runs down through the middle of that fifty acre farm to this day.

Seventeen

Brown Eyes

One of the crops we raised on our farm that did require a lot of hard work was sugar beets from which sugar is made. This crop, in some instances, was cared for partially by migrant workers.

Several different years we hired Mexican people to care for our beets. One such family was from San Antonio, Texas, by the name of Garcia. When they came out into the field to work, the whole family would come, about nine or ten in all from the baby up to the two older boys, Raymond and Marion. I really liked those folks. I especially liked to hear the boys play their twelve-string guitars and sing their Spanish songs in the evenings after work. They were living in the McDurmond house at that time.

Raymond sold me his guitar one fall before they left to go back to Texas. Several of us boys enjoyed trying to learn to play it over the next year or two. It was common to find it standing near the stairway door propped in a corner when not in use. The last day it played was when it happen to tip into the path of the door just as it slammed shut!

One day while I was out with the little tractor cultivating beets, Raymond came over and offered me a Mexican tamale. I had never seen or heard of a tamale before, but I was game to try it. It was wrapped in paper, so I stuck it in my shirt pocket. When I got home that evening, I got up enough courage to taste it. As I remember, it had ground up meat in it with lots of spices, then was wrapped in corn husks, and cooked. It was not uncommon to see the makin's of those things hanging on the clothesline in their backyard. The light-colored corn husks were very visible from the road.

The next day Raymond came over and asked me how I liked the tamale. I think I might have stretched the truth a little and said it was okay, 'cause I didn't want to offend him. I just wasn't used to food with so many spices. At that time we didn't have any Mexican restaurants that I knew of in our part of the country. I have eaten tamales since then, and they are not all that bad. Actually, I like Mexican food now.

I hadn't mentioned this before, but that Garcia family did have a teenage daughter with long black hair and snappy brown eyes. I sort of enjoyed taking the little tractor out into the field to cultivate when they were all out there working. As I think back on it now, I wouldn't be a bit surprised if that girl didn't turn out to be a farmer, because she sure seemed to be taking more than a casual interest in the tractor I was driving. I didn't blame her for watching, 'cuz it was a pretty neat little tractor.

Eighteen

Made In the Shade

Now getting back to the mundane stuff. I will explain a little about the beet crop itself.

The beet seed was planted with a bean drill that sowed four to six rows at a time. When the little beet plants got about one and a half inches high, the real work began. Since they were sown in this manner, the little plants were too close together to be left growing that way. That required two operations.

First, one of the older persons would go along and block the beets, and then usually one of us younger ones would crawl along behind on our hands and knees thinning them. I might add, that could get pretty old after a while, because some of our fields were from 1\4 to 1\2 mile long!

Blocking was done with a hoe about eight inches wide. Once that was done, there would be anywhere from one to four little plants in each hill. So the person coming along thinning, would pull up all but one seedling in each hill. The purpose of this system was so that the beet plant would have plenty of room to expand.

After several years of this back-breaking work, Pa decided to do some experimenting. He, along with my older brothers, came up with a pretty neat idea. They decided to build a machine that would make thinning easier.

This machine moved along real slow across the beet field carrying four people. They started with a Model T Ford engine, added two old Chevrolet transmissions, and a Model T Ford truck differential. They coupled these all together in an old car frame. Then out from the rear, they built a platform about seven or eight feet wide and about six feet long. This platform was suspended above the ground about twelve inches. It was wide enough for four people to lay face down, side by side, with their arms reaching through the space provided, and a canvas band for resting your forehead.

One of the younger kids drove the machine straddle two rows of beets, as the other four of us rode along, facing the ground thinning as we went. Wow, what a blessing that was! The platform also had a canopy, so we wouldn't have to lay in the hot sun. That invention really made thinning beets much more enjoyable.

We usually had one of the other younger kids walking along behind this machine to catch any of the hills of beets that might have been missed. If one of us knew that we were not keeping up, we would holler, "Check, Don," if Don happened to be the one following, bringing up the rear. Then he would look for the hill that we missed and take care of it. Occasionally, one of us would switch off with that weary person who had been walking along behind. It was always a nice break to be able to get off your feet and lay down in the shade of canopy for a while. Pa seemed to always be looking for ways to make the farm work a little more pleasant.

As the beets continued growing, the weeds also began to grow. So before long it was time to hoe the beets. This was much easier than thinning. Several of us with hoe in hand, would each take a row and fan out, going back and forth across the field until all the weeds were cut down.

I know this is repetitious, but there was a lot of work connected with this crop, and the hardest part was still to come. Along about the middle of October, the sugar beets had grown as much as they were going to. Many of the other crops were already harvested, so we were able to give most of our attention to the beets.

A sugar beet can get to be a pretty good size. Eight to ten inches in diameter and ten to twelve inches long was not uncommon. Of course, many were smaller, but even so, because of the dirt that clung to them, they were still heavy to work with. At harvest time they were pretty firmly rooted in the ground, and for that reason we didn't just go along and pull them up by hand.

They have very modern equipment nowadays, but back then it required a lot of hand work. First of all, to get the beets loosened up from the soil, we used what was called a beet lifter. At that time it was horse drawn, similar to a single plow. But instead of turning the soil over, it would slice through the soil along side the row, and just lift the plant enough so the roots were pulled loose.

As soon as there were a few rows lifted, a group of us would go along, each taking two rows, and pull the beets by grabbing them around the tops (leaves). With one in each hand, the workers would strike them together, knocking off the excess dirt. We would then throw them in piles with the tops facing the same way. The two rows of piles would be about eight feet apart, the full length of the field. Down between those rows of beets, we would pull an A-frame float with a team of horses or a small tractor to level the ground.

The next part of the job was to come along with the beet knives and cut the tops off and throw the beets in another pile on the leveled area. Those beet knives were shaped like a short machete, with a curved hook at the outer end. If you were right handed, you would stand over the pile of beets, reach out and hook the knife into the thick part of the beet, then raise it up and grab it with your left hand. Real

158

quick-like, you would whack off the top and a bit of the crown, throwing the beet in another pile to be hauled to the sugar factory.

By the time I was old enough to drive a truck on the road, we had a 1934 Chevy one and a half ton truck. We would drive through the field alongside the rows of piles, and with a beet fork (about the size of a large scoop shovel) would pitch the beets up over the sides into the truck to be hauled to the sugar factory. Our truck could come out of the field with between six and eight ton per load when the ground was dry.

The only sugar factory in the area was the PIONEER SUGAR COMPANY in Caro, located about eight miles southwest of our place. Sometimes I would have to wait in line to get unloaded. Our truck rack had sideboards. The left one would hinge down, and the rack itself was built to hinge sideways. So to unload at the factory, they had a large set of chains with rings in them that hooked into the right side of the rack and picked it up until the beets all rolled out into the big hopper.

We always had to weigh in with the load and then weigh out when we left. The beets would be run through a set of screens to remove the excess dirt, leaves, etc.. This "tare," as it was called, would all be dumped back into the truck before we weighed out. The company would pay for the beets on the basis of the net weight.

As sugar beet growers, we were also able to buy sugar direct from the factory at a discount. Being a large family, we used a lot of sugar in canning, as well as many other things, so we took advantage of the offer. I can remember one year in particular, probably about 1940. Pa and I went down with the truck and brought home one-half ton of white sugar in ten, one hundred pound bags. I carried it all upstairs and stored it in the hallway. That kept us in sugar for quite a while. This gave us a good supply to dip into when we needed to fill the bin down in the kitchen. But it was a little bit of a trick to keep the gritty sugar swept up so we didn't track it around with our bare feet as we came to and from the three bedrooms that led off from this hallway.

To make harvesting even more of a trial, there would be times that the snow would come before we got the beets harvested. If we were planning to leave the topped beets in the field for an extended period of time, we would cover the piles with beet tops. When I say tops, I mean the beet leaves which are still attached to a slice of the beet. One year I remember in particular, the snow was so deep you couldn't even see the piles from a distance. That year we had to take a shovel and dig down through the snow to uncover them before we could load them on the truck or wagon.

In 1938 it was so wet we couldn't get the tractor and lifter into the field, so Lawrence Smith, a cousin, brought his team of mules over and together with my team, King and Molly, we sloshed through the mud, lifting the six acres we still had in the ground.

Nineteen

Timber-r-r-r-r

(A Flashback)

The December sky was kinda murky and gray with an occasional flurry of snow floating down out of the northwest. All the livestock in the barnyard had congregated back in under the edge of the big straw stack. A few months before we had blown in all of our wheat and oat straw from the threshing machine, up, over, and around the cattle-run shed. What a neat place that was for all the livestock to get back out of the cold wind.

With a few inches of dry snow still on the ground from the blizzard we had had just a few days before, John, Roy, and I decided to take the big sleighs and get a load of wood for the furnace. It was located underneath the dining room and would burn either coal or wood, and so we used both.

While I gathered up a couple of axes and a cross-cut saw, the boys harnessed up Molly and King (King was Molly's four year old colt, a beautiful Belgium about four hundred pounds heavier than his mom and worked nicely with her.)

In no time we were gliding along down the lane toward the woods. As we made the last turn in the lane, a big rooster pheasant burst up out of the fence row and went sailing off into the tall, dead grass along the rail fence.

Somehow, I guess he knew that the bird hunting season was over for that year. What a thrill to be out in the woods! Even if it meant work, there was still something exciting about being back there among those huge maple, elm, and oak trees. We zig-zagged back through the woods until we came upon a few trees that were dead or nearly so.

With the bitter cold wind whistling through the tall trees, me being the little guy, I found myself a nice big maple to stand behind while Roy and John cut down the first tree. Back and forth, back and forth with the two-man crosscut saw. As they got it almost cut through, a big gust of wind came along and finished the job.

"Timber-r-r-r-r!" cried Roy. Crash! It came thundering to the earth. The boys took a few minutes break, then grabbed up the old trusty crosscut and began whacking it up into stove-length pieces, while I loaded them onto the sleighs one piece at a time.

We made our way back down the lane toward the house with sounds of the clippity-clop of the horses hooves on the frozen ground and the jingle of the harnesses being carried by the cold wind. Roy drove the team and sleighs past the chicken house and around between the smokehouse and the back porch. With a slight tug on the left reign, he swung King and Molly right up to the basement window, whose frame was already badly scarred from big blocks of wood that had missed their mark a few times before. We weren't long in pitching our load into the furnace room, which still had a small pile of soft coal over in one corner. As the boys put the team away, I began doing the evening chores.

The next morning it was still too nasty to be outside, so the three of us went into the corn crib and shelled corn for the cattle and chickens. The crib was a long, narrow building with slotted boards on all sides. By slotted, I mean the boards used were about four inches in width and spaced about an inch apart so air could pass through to help dry the ears of corn.

Corn was used for the hogs, cattle, and chickens. For the hogs, we just fed them the whole ear and let them do their own shelling as they ate it. For the cattle, sometimes we would grind up the whole ear in with oats or barley. For the chickens, some of it was ground up into mash and some cracked by running the shelled corn lightly through the hammer mill. This was called scratch feed.

Since it was usually on snowy or rainy days that we shelled corn, one of our hired men coined a phrase for the occasion. He said, "More rain, more shelly corn." And we usually had a "shelly corn" day about every four to six weeks during the winter months. A by-product of these shelly corn days was a nice, big pile of dry corn cobs. A little handful made wonderful kindling for starting fires in the coal or wood stove.

Twenty

Sweet Smells of Silage

We raised quite a lot of corn on our farm. Some of it was harvested early for silage, just as the kernels of corn were in the dough stage. A good way to test it was to push your thumbnail into an ear of corn. If it didn't squirt the milk into your eye, you knew it was just right for silage. That's what was called the dough stage. What wasn't cut for silage was left to ripen completely.

Ripe corn was cut into bundles with a corn binder, and then shocked up in the field. Sometimes it would be left there until winter before it was brought in to be run through a corn shredder. This machine separated the ears from the stalks. The ears would be conveyed up into a wagon or truck, and the stalks were chopped up and blown into the barn to be used for cattle feed during the cold winter months when the pasture fields were laying dormant.

I especially liked to help with the early cutting. This corn was also cut with a corn binder, and tied in bundles. But instead of shocking the corn in the field, we just came through with the horses and wagon and loaded it on to be hauled up to the silo filler.

The silo on our farm was built of concrete staves, twelve feet wide and thirty-five feet high. It was used to store feed for the cattle. To fill the silo required a silo filler. This was a machine which was powered by a large tractor. We threw the bundles of corn onto a conveyor, and they were carried right along and into a set of fast turning knives, which were also fastened to a large blower. On the side of the blower was a long pipe, about the size of a six-inch stove pipe, which went up the full height of the silo. The power of the blower was so strong that it would propel the chopped corn stalks all the way up and into the silo. As the silage increased in depth, it was necessary to have two or three men walking around in there, tramping it down to help prevent spoilage.

It was so much fun being down inside the silo. It had a strange hollow sound when it was empty, maybe like being in a big barrel. As the big Model "D" tractor began to rev up with the heavy belts slapping against themselves, we could hear the wind whistling through the blower pipe that dangled down into the silo. Every few seconds someone would throw in another huge bundle of green corn. "Wh-u-u-u-mg!" would groan the machine. In a couple of seconds, a fresh dose of sweet smelling silage came floating down from above. If all went well, we could fill the silo in one day. However, after a couple of days the silage would settle about five or six feet, and we would crank up and fill it to the top one more time.

All through the winter months we had nice smelling corn silage to feed our cattle. Just the aroma of that fermented, chopped up green corn almost made us hungry. We would give each cow a scoop shovelful in their manger, and then sprinkle a couple of quarts of ground grain on top of it. Boy, did the cows ever go after that stuff!

Part Four

1937 - 1944

One

Deer Tracks

Pa and most of us boys liked to hunt. As each of us became old enough, we were taught to handle a gun properly. For many years our hunting was limited to pheasants, and occasionally rabbits. Pheasants were quite plentiful then, and so that seemed to be the big thing when the season rolled around. The small game season would open on the 15th of October. By that time the grain and some of the corn was harvested, which meant there was plenty of feed and cover for the birds. They also liked the protection of the mature sugar beets, and that made a favorite place to hunt. Phil Seeger from Birmingham, Michigan, as well as some other visitors from the city, would often come up and hunt on our farm.

I suppose it was along about 1935 that Pa and Ma bought the gravel farm three and one half miles south of Colwood. And since the land was on the light side, Pa and the older boys talked of getting a flock of sheep to put up there to pasture. Through a little inquiring, Pa heard of a farmer in North Michigan, near South Branch, who had a flock of sheep for sale. He had made arrangements to purchase the whole flock and had planned to go with the truck around the last of October to bring them home.

But a few days before they were to go after them, Alvin called and said to Pa, "What do you say we wait a week or so and maybe we can bring back a couple extra?" By "a couple extra," he meant deer. Deer season opened the 15th of November.

I, being a little too young at that time, had to stay home and take care of the cattle, etc., but Pa and Alvin got together a party of six or eight guys. I believe that first group consisted of Pa, Alvin, Elden, John, Clifford Smith (our brother-in-law), Lawrence Smith (our cousin), and maybe Carl Smith (Pa's cousin).

Since they had no idea of where to go, Clifford said he had an uncle and aunt who lived near Mikado, which was in good deer hunting territory. They made arrangements to go there and took a big tent for their sleeping quarters.

The day they arrived it was cold and very windy. Clifford's uncle almost insisted that they not try to stay in the tent, but to come on into the house and sleep where it was warm. But Pa, not wanting to impose on anyone, suggested that they just set up the tent in their backyard. Everyone agreed and pitched in to set up. With the echo of the last tent stake being driven into the ground, they all lugged their blankets and sleeping gear inside and prepared for a nice, peaceful rest.

But sometime during the night, the big tent began to lunge and surge, straining under the force of that cold, north wind. It became apparent that those little tent pegs would not hold out much longer. Sure enough, pop, pop, pop, as each of the tent pegs flipped out of the frozen ground, collapsing the whole kit and caboodle. One by one those mighty hunters came crawling out from under the heavy canvas. Out of desperation, they finally agreed to go inside after all.

Well, that turned out to be quite an experience for all them. I believe Clifford was the only one to get a buck that year, but for each of them it was an adventure they would not soon forget. That was the beginning of what was to become an annual event for our family--deer hunting in the north woods.

When the next hunting season rolled around, I was about fifteen. Since Fred and Dick were now old enough to do the chores, I asked Pa if I could go with them this time, and he said I could. Having only one gun, the old double-barrel .12 gauge shotgun, he let me use that, and he borrowed a rifle from Clifford.

This particular year we had made arrangements to stay with Roy Crosby, another one of Clifford's uncles, who lived in an old house near Hubbard Lake not far from where they hunted the first year. I don't remember whether Alvin went or not. I believe our party consisted of Pa, Elden, Carl Smith, Roy Crosby, Clifford, and me.

We arrived up there the night before the season opened. Roy was waiting for us, and we unloaded all of our gear and enjoyed a good supper that had been prepared. After the dishes were washed, we all sat around the wood heater telling stories until late into the evening. Finally, so we would all have a good night's rest, we began one by one to climb the old rickety stairs into the loft. We all slept in this one big room. My bunk was right opposite Roy's, and I was amused at his bed covers. Among the many blankets was also what looked like a mini-mattress about three inches thick. I don't know how he got any sleep under all that load, but I'm sure he at least kept warm.

In what seemed to be a very short time the alarm rang. The temperature had dipped pretty low that night, so we could see our breath as we climbed out of bed and into our woolen hunting clothes. Down the stairs we filed. Roy had bacon frying, coffee perking, and was mixing up the pancake batter. I can't explain the excitement I felt as we all dug into those pancakes and bacon. Breakfast over and the dishes washed up, we began bundling up for the day ahead. I began thinking to myself, *In no time at all I'll be standing out there somewhere in the big north woods waiting to get my very first glimpse of a real live deer.*

It was still pitchdark outside as we got ready to leave the house. Each of us gathered up our hunting gear. Mine consisted of a double-barrel .12 gauge shotgun, six buck shot shells, six rifled slugs, a small ax that hung from my belt, a hunting knife, and a short piece of rope for dragging in my deer. We all climbed into Elden's '37 Oldsmobile and headed down the dirt road. There was several inches of fresh snow on the ground, and there had been no cars down this road since the snow came. As we drove about half a mile west, then turning north toward Hubbard Lake, Roy began to lay out the hunting strategy for the day. Since he knew the area well, we paid close attention.

We were cruising right along toward the lake and, as we came up over the top of a ridge, he said, "This would be a good place for Pa Smith." So Elden pulled off to the side of the road and let Pa out.

As we continued on down the road, Roy looked at me and said, "There's a good place for you right down at the foot of this hill." He then added, "There's a deer runway that crosses the road right here, and if you will stand there all day, I know you will see deer." That sounded good to me, so I jumped out of the car with gun and ammo in hand.

As I watched the red taillights disappear over the next hill, I realized that deer season had finally arrived. Then it dawned on me, *I am here in this big woods all alone in the dark, and I'm only 15!*

I walked back off the road a short distance and stood next to a snow-covered scotch pine and waited for daylight. Elden had dropped Carl off about halfway between Pa and me, and he, Roy, and Clifford went on further north. Before long I began to sense slight evidences of dawn. It was just a short while before I could discern the outline of the trees across the road and was able to get the lay of the land by looking up and down the road. Not knowing the first thing about deer hunting, I decided to try different things. I found out in a short time that I was not going to be a "still" hunter, because my feet got cold too easily.

I stood for a while in one spot, looking back and forth through the trees, watching for signs of movement. As soon as I started getting cold, I would quietly walk back into the woods a few hundred yards, then back up near the road again.

Just as traces of daylight were beginning to appear, I happened to be looking up the road north from where I stood, and in the gray dawn I saw what I took to be three or four goats jumping across the road ditch. I thought, *That's neat.* Then all of a sudden it struck me, *Hey, those are deer!* (You see, I had never seen real deer in the wild.) Now I was beginning to get excited. Wow, seeing deer before full daylight! But then I remembered what Roy said before I got out of the car that morning, "If you stand right there all day, you will see deer."

But as I said, I couldn't stand in one spot for hours on end, so whenever I began to get a little chilled, I would take off walking, all the time hoping I wouldn't scare away a prize deer. Before the day was out, I had even built a fire to keep warm. I couldn't see any reason for freezing to death, even though there was the risk of scaring away the deer. I found out a few years later that building a fire does not scare deer. I didn't have much lunch that day, because I had been nibbling on my bologna sandwich long before noon. And all that was left of my Baby Ruth was a wrapper.

It was now getting along toward evening, the sun had fallen behind the tall trees, and that north Michigan chill had settled in. I had already seen twenty to twenty-five deer so far, and although that was pretty exciting in itself, I would have liked to have seen some with horns. So I decided to go back to my original stomping ground just off the edge of the road and stand there until dark, or until Elden, Clifford, and Roy came along to pick me up.

I just stood there, facing east across the road in the direction of the deer runway, where I could see the trail disappear into the thicket. It was now beginning to get dusk, and I was getting colder by the minute, but was determined to hang on until nightfall. I stood there for quite awhile with my old .12 gauge under my arm and my hands in my coat pocket. Then all of a sudden--there it was--a movement in the bushes across the road about fifty yards away!

Sure enough, out walked a nice big doe, then another, then another, until four or five walked out. Without seeing me, they just circled back into the brush on that side of the road. Now I had been told by Roy and some of the other men, that if you see a doe, you are liable to see a buck following some distance behind.

Based on that much information, I raised my gun and aimed in the direction of the deer and waited. I had a buck shot shell in one barrel and a rifled slug in the other. The theory being, that I would have a better chance of hitting a deer with the buck shot, then if I needed another shot to finish him off, the slug would be better for that.

So there I stood, shivering from the cold and from buck fever, with the gun to my shoulder, pointed toward that little clearing where I had seen the other deer come out. My arms were getting tired from holding the gun in one position so long--then it happened. The bushes began moving again in that same location and here came my nice four-point buck pushing his way out into the clearing. He evidently had not even noticed me, but did just as the others had done, he circled back into the woods.

As he got broadside to me, I squeezed the trigger and down he went. I was pretty nervous, shaky, and wondering, *What do I do now?* I had never killed a big animal like that before, but I remembered something else Roy told us all. "Never walk up to a deer to put your ID tag on him until you are sure he is dead."

Deciding not to take any chances, I backed off a few feet and put a slug through his shoulders. Then I proceeded to cut his throat, so he would bleed thoroughly. By this time, I was really shaking, cold, excited, and a little proud of myself. It was also getting quite dark, and wanting to keep it somewhat of a secret, I just left my buck laying there and walked back across the road. I stayed in my original spot and waited for Elden and the others to come along. In a few minutes, I heard the Olds coming up over the hill. As they came to a stop at my crossing, Elden hollered out in a doubting tone of voice, "Hey, Bill, where's your buck?"

I said, "It's laying right over there in the woods."

"Oh, sure it is," he answered.

"Well, just come and see."

When he and the others laid their eyes on my nice four-point stretched out there behind the stump, they could hardly believe it! We dragged him out to the road, loaded him onto the fender of the car, and headed on up the next hill to pick up the others. Carl was the first to get in and then we drove to where Pa was waiting. I could see the surprised look on his face as he started to climb into the back seat. Carl said to Pa, "Here's the guy, here's the guy," as he pointed in my direction. Pa was sure pleased to have me get a buck on my first trip. I was the youngest in our party and happened to be the only one to get one that year.

Well, that experience was my introduction to what was to become a very pleasurable yearly event. In the years that followed, our hunting parties included, besides Pa and my brothers, Clifford, Charles Dibbley, Ed Roush, Willie Bryde, and Erwin Whitfield. We hunted all around Hulbert and Pickford in the Upper Peninsula of Michigan, as well as the Hubbard Lake area.

Bill with his four-point buck

I mentioned previously about whether or not building fires interferes with deer sightings. Let me recount an incident that happened to me a few years later.

It was probably about the third day of deer hunting in the Upper Peninsula of Michigan, ten miles east of Pickford. I believe our party consisted of Alvin, Elden, Cilfford, Willie Bryde, Charles Dibbley, Erwin Whitfield, and me. Paul Hart, a pastor friend of the Dibbley's from Pickford, hunted with us part of the time.

Late one afternoon, Alvin and Elden decided to go back to one of their favorite spots along the lake and hunt until dark. "That's a good idea," I said, "I think I'll go along and stop off at my favorite place." This place was special, because a couple of days earlier I had seen a deer with the largest rack of horns I had ever seen in the wild. So the three of us gathered up our gear and headed down the little dirt road that led into the big woods.

I stopped off at my place, and they continued on, maybe a quarter of a mile further. I soon got situated on the edge of the clearing, just a few yards from an old, dilapidated hunting cabin. The setting was a deer hunters dream. From my location, I was looking off across a clearing, probably 75 feet wide into a very thick stand of poplars. About 4:30 in the afternoon that November sun began to sink down behind the trees, and with that the north Michigan chill began to settle in also.

I stood pretty quietly for as long as I could, because I knew my brothers didn't appreciate all the racket I make when I build a fire. Finally, I had no choice. I was getting cold. Unhooking my little camp ax from my belt, I began to whack off chips from an old dead pine stump. *CHOP, CHOP, CHOP.* The wood was very dry, so in minutes I had a nice fire started. It felt so good I decided to just stand over it until I got thawed out. (By the way, that's an awkward position to be in if a nice buck shows up.)

In less than five minutes while looking off into the poplars with smoke filled eyes, I saw an unbelievable sight--not one, but six or seven white-tailed deer, marching as if by command toward my fire. Knowing that the best way to spook a deer is to make a quick move, I stood perfectly still, while being suffocated with pine wood smoke. Here they came in perfect single-file down the little narrow path through the thick poplars. The lead deer, a young spike-horn, came right up to the edge of the clearing in full view and stopped dead in his tracks. And with that, all the others stopped also.

If you have never been in a similar position, you can't imagine what a tense situation this creates. I knew if I even made the slightest move, the show would be over. It's hard to explain the feeling, having a wild animal standing approximately twenty feet away, staring straight into your eyes without moving a muscle.

In what seemed like forever, but was probably no more than forty seconds, an astonishing thing happened. My beautiful spike-horn pivoted on his hind legs 180 degrees, now facing in the direction he had come from. I wish I had on video what happened the moment he did that. Every single one of the other deer made exactly the same maneuver, as if they were somehow all hooked together mechanically. What a sight!

Incredibly, instead of charging off 90 miles an hour, they just leisurely walked back down the trail. I remembered what our host, Mr. Edgerly, said before we left camp that morning. "We're about out of 'sausage,' so if you see a deer, shoot it whether it is a buck or a doe." So as the deer began walking away, I lined up my .38-55 Winchester with a little clearing, then when the last deer walked through, I pulled the trigger--BANG!--and down he went.

I'll have to say, I did feel a little proud of myself for getting a deer. However, my greatest concern was what my older brothers were thinking about all the racket. I could imagine them saying, "That kid is not content to drive all the deer out of the county with that silly ax, he's also got to do a little target practicing, too."

I did walk over to get a closer look at my beautiful spike-horn, but realizing that the boys would soon be coming in for the day, I just left him lay until they got there. In less than thirty minutes, here came Alvin and Elden trudging up the trail. As they came into view, Elden said, "Bill, was that you shooting?"

"That was me," I answered, with a slight grin.

"And what was you shooting at?"

"Well, let me show you," I replied, as I started leading them over about 75 feet into the poplar thicket. When they saw that magnificent creature laying there with his shiny, brown coat and stubby, little horns, they could scarcely believe their eyes.

As darkness settled in that evening, the three of us took turns dragging our deer back to the camp. As it happened, Erwin Whitfield also got one that day, so that replenished our "sausage" supply again for several days. After supper we all went out into the garage, and Mr. Edgerly helped us dress out the two deer.

That settled it once and for all as far as I'm concerned --building a campfire does not scare away deer. Quite the opposite.

Two

Lost Hunter

The following year in that same general area, we hunted again with Roy Crosby who was very familiar with the territory, and we left it up to him to choose the areas we would hunt. It was about the third day of the season and up to this time none of us had gotten a deer. Roy suggested we go over on the plains and hunt that afternoon. The plains are not what you might think. It was not a nice big open field, but was hundreds of acres of small trees about twenty-five feet high.

As we loaded up and drove out there, winding our way down the little dirt road, Roy was beginning to give us our assignments. We pulled into a little clearing and all climbed out of the car.

Roy then led us all over onto somewhat of a ridge and pointed off across the plains. "Do you see those two big pine trees over there?" he asked us. They were in plain view to everyone, because they stood twice as high as the other trees around there. He then said, "We are going to spread out, with maybe one hundred yards between us, and make a drive in that direction and meet there under those two trees."

Now I had visualized in my mind that those two trees were standing out on a little ridge all by themselves in a clearing, and so would be easily recognized when I got there. I was the youngest one in the bunch again, but thought it wouldn't be that difficult to find those two trees, even if we got separated on our way over there.

We started fanning out from each other and moving forward through the woods as quietly as we could. I was where I could see Roy for a little while and just a short way into the woods I heard him say, "There's one."

As he spoke, he dropped to one knee and fired about four shots as fast as he could rack his .32 Winchester. But whatever he was shooting at got away. So here we went again, off across the country. By this time no one else was in view. Now I was on my own, trying to remember the instructions. "Don't walk too fast. If you think you are lost, you are likely to walk in circles." Unknowingly, I began to walk faster and faster and before long I did come to two big pine trees. But instead of them being out in the open like I thought they were supposed to be, they were standing right among all those shorter hardwoods. Now I was confused. *Are these the two pines I was supposed to come to or have I discovered two others?*

I stood there under those big trees, wondering. I thought to myself, *If those were the right trees, how come I'm the only one here?* So I just waited, and listened. About the only sounds were an occasional screech of a blue jay. Now my heart was beginning to pound a little. I must be lost. But how could I be? I thought I had come on a pretty straight line through the woods. But since I couldn't hear anyone walking, I now was convinced I was lost.

My first instinct was to get moving. *But which way?* I wondered. I decided to continue on as nearly as I could in the same general direction that I had been going. I hurried along through the woods for ten to fifteen minutes, hoping I would see or at least hear someone. Then I remembered that I had heard several years before, "If you ever become lost in the woods, don't keep running. Just sit down where you are and wait."

So that's what I decided to do. There was thick scrub oak and poplar trees all around me, and you couldn't see far in any direction. All of a sudden a terrible thought entered my head, *I may have to spend the night out here.* It was already beginning to cool down as it always does late in the day in the north woods. One of my first concerns was if I had matches to build a fire with? I dug through my pockets and, thankfully, found some. My little camp ax was dangling from my belt, so I made plans to start chipping off slivers from a big charred pine stump that stood nearby.

Then I thought, *before I give up completely, I'll just start hollering as loud as I can and maybe someone will hear me.* Every four or five seconds I let out a war-hoop as loud as I could. But the only answer I got was my own echo ringing back through the big woods. Then I had another idea. *I guess I'll shoot into that stump a few times and see if that gets anyone's attention.* Boom! Boom! the sound rang out, as I shot into the stump with my old .12 gauge shotgun. Then I just waited for several more minutes, but no response. Sure was quiet out there as the chilly night air started settling in.

I decided to try hollering one more time. After about four or five yelps, I thought I heard a voice. I listened. *Am I delirious or is that really an honest to goodness human voice?* Very faintly I began to hear Elden calling my name, and I was able to identify which direction the voice came from. It was in the general area through which I had trudged earlier in the afternoon. I gathered up my stuff and beat it off in that direction. In a short time, I was with the rest of our party. Where do you suppose they were all standing? Yep, right under the two pine trees I had seen earlier in the afternoon. Boy, was I glad to be back with the gang! Since it was beginning to get along toward dusk, we all headed back to our camp. That turned out to be quite an eventful hunting trip, even though we came home again without anyone connecting with a buck!

Three

Excited Forest Ranger

It was along about the time of the deer hunting season in 1939, that John, Ruth, and family came up from Birmingham to visit us. The few previous years he had been hunting in the upper peninsula of Michigan with Bruce Shaw, his boss. While they were there at our house, John asked me if I would like to join him in a hunting trip to the Hubbard Lake area, and I said, "I sure would!" This lake was nestled right in among some of the best deer hunting territory in that part of Michigan. So we made plans to rent a cabin on the lake for a week. A man who John knew, by the name of John Weir from Detroit, owned several cabins there, and we called him to reserve one for the first week of deer season.

Boy, I really counted the days leading up to the 15th of November. I got all my hunting gear together days in advance, cleaned and oiled my .12 gauge shotgun, and bought a couple of boxes of buck shot and one box of rifled slugs. It was about a one hundred and fifty mile ride up there, so we planned to leave early on the morning of the 14th.

The typical deer hunting chill was in the air the morning John pulled into our yard with his big red, twelve-cylinder

Lincoln Zephyr. What a spiffy bus! We were going hunting in style this time. I had stayed on ready, counting the days and hours, and we weren't long at all in getting my stuff loaded up.

As we pulled out of the driveway early that morning, a few light fluffy snowflakes bounced off the hood of the car. Boy, what excitement! I don't know whether you call it hunting fever or what, but it seems to me that it comes pretty close to being an addiction. Just the thought of taking your flashlight and trudging out before daylight in search of a fresh deer trail -- Wow!

By the time we pulled into Bay City, we were both ready for a good plate of bacon, eggs, and coffee. Between Bay City and Pinconning the light flurries seemed to be a little more serious, and by the time we drove down to Mr. Weir's general store on the lake, the snow was really coming down.

Mr. Weir and his wife were glad to see us, and after a short greeting, he took us to our cabin. The gas heater had been on for a couple of hours so the little two-room frame cabin was nice and cozy.

We had planned to do most of our own cooking at the cabin while we were there, but this first day to save time we walked over to the lodge and had a hot plate lunch. After lunch we finished settling in to our new home, then spent the rest of the day driving around the area looking for places to hunt.

John had not hunted here before, and I suggested we go back and try the area where I got my buck on our first trip up there on the little gravel road south of the lake. Early the next morning, after finishing off a plate of pancakes and sausage, we got dressed for the cold day ahead; red plaid hunting pants and jacket, red cap, red jersey gloves with the trigger finger missing, and high-top leather boots. John's gun was a .12 gauge Browning automatic, and mine a .12 gauge Remington automatic. Extra equipment included a small camp ax, hunting knife, compass, and a short piece of clothes line rope.

It was still dark when we pulled away from our camp that first morning. Wow! It's almost impossible to describe the feeling of excitement. John swung his big Lincoln around onto the winding dirt road that led out to the Hubbard Lake road. As those bright headlights cast their beams through the woods while making our turns along the way, we both strained our eyes watching for little glassy eyes looking back at us. Before long we were pulling into a small clearing not far from where we were going to hunt. Quietly unloading our equipment and easing the door shut, we headed through the woods to our favorite spot. John went one way, and I went another.

In a short time, traces of daylight began to filter into the thickness around us so that we could sorta get the lay of the land. Settling in behind a little clump of bushes on a large broken off tree limb, I began my vigil, sitting with my .12 gauge automatic under my arm. I waited for the first big buck to come sneaking out of the thicket. But for some reason, we didn't see the action that I had experienced in previous years. We finished out the first day without even seeing one single deer.

On the second day, we went back to the same general area on the gravel road south of the lake. The weather had begun to warm up quite a bit, and the woods were sort of quiet (deer move in cold weather). Along about lunch time John came out to where I had been hunting all morning, and said, "Have you seen any deer?"

I said, "No, just a lot of fresh tracks."

After eating a ham sandwich and a couple of cookies, we poured each of us a cup of hot coffee from our thermos and just relaxed up against a big pine tree. The sun was beaming down onto the floor of the woods, making it feel more like August instead of November. Since we had left our car down the road a ways from where we were hunting, we decided to walk out in that direction just for a change. The dead twigs and leaves crackled under foot as we made our way down the trail to the road. As we approached the ditch bank, we stopped a minute to be sure we didn't spook any deer that might be out in the clearing.

Just as we were about to step out into the road, we heard a car break up over the hill just south of us, and was he traveling! When he saw us standing there, he slammed on his breaks, with gravel stones flying. Then rolling down the car window, he hollered, "Why aren't you fellas up there fighting that fire?"

"We didn't know there was one," we answered.

He said, "Follow me."

Noticing the funny little badge on his sleeve, we responded, "Yes, sir." He was the Alcona County conservation officer, so guess what we did? We had no choice, because he waited until we got our guns and equip- ment loaded in the car. You should have seen John and I in our big Lincoln Zephyr snaking up the crooked mountain road behind the Chevy ranger car. Up, up and up we went trailing a long cloud of dust. As we reached the top of the mountain, we could see that the fire had already burned over two or three acres and was moving fast as it roared down the south side of the slope.

Jumping out of the car, the ranger didn't say, "Would you guys like to help us?" He just handed each of us a shovel, and we joined the other couple dozen hunters that had already been recruited. We began flogging our way down the mountain ahead of the flames, which were being fed by the very dry underbrush and needles. In about an hour, we had the fire under control, and by that time were ready for a ' cool drink break. We handed in our fire fighting tools, drove back off the mountain, and over to Weir's lodge. Flopping into a booth back in the corner, we each guzzled down an ice cold bottle of Pepsi Cola!

The next day dawned bright and sunny and was not looking too promising for deer hunting, so we decided to rent a row boat and tour Hubbard Lake, one stroke at a time. The water was calm that day as we paddled along close to the shore, exploring as we went. We hoped we would at least see some deer from the boat, but on warm days they stay pretty quiet, laying up in the hardwoods. The week went by without either of us seeing many deer, much less getting a buck.

Saturday morning we loaded up our hunting gear and left for home. If shooting a buck deer was what it took to make a successful deer hunt, then I guess John and I failed. But money cannot buy the enjoyment we had just being together, sharing laughs, and sometimes just plain tom foolery (silly carrying on). John and I were good friends as well as brothers.

Four

Gloomy Clouds of War

In 1939 when I was 17, World War II broke out. Things were going along pretty much as usual on the farm, but we began to enter into a period of stress and uncertainty as far as our nation was concerned. Franklin Roosevelt was president and many of our young men were being called up for military duty. The draft age was 18 or older, so I was not quite old enough to be drafted. My cousin, Charles Smith, was one of the first in our community to be called. Although I was too young to go, I became very interested in the war itself. At the beginning, our nation was involved with our allies against Germany.

Almost every night after the chores were done, I would come in and sit by the radio and listen to the war news. (This was before television). I would hear Walter Cronkite in New York, Eric Severied in London, and Wm L. White in Helsinki. They would all give a description of what was taking place from the sources available to them. There were times when the reports from Eric in London would be interrupted while German V2 rockets were screaming over head. (These were the first jet-propelled projectiles used by the Germans against England and France.) The very thought of those newly developed weapons struck terror into the hearts of the people across the English channel.

The war dragged on, and in 1940 I became old enough for the draft and did go to Detroit for my physical. But the government began to defer draft age boys who were actively engaged in farming, because of the critical need for food production. However, this was not a very comfortable position to be in either. When some of the other boys came home on furlough, they would look at you as a draft dodger. Two of my younger brothers did serve in the military a few years later: Fred in the European theater in World War II, and Don in the Pacific during the Korean War.

Because so many of our nation's resources were being used up for the military, our government initiated the rationing of several commodities, such as: gasoline, tires, batteries, sugar, shoes, boots, etc. They also discontinued building cars and trucks for civilian use and didn't start up again until the war officially ended in 1945. The government issued ration stamps to every family throughout the country based on their eligibility.

I've mentioned before how much respect we all had for our Pa, but this little incident I'm going to relate will help to show what I mean.

If you wanted to buy an item that was rationed, you had to have a stamp as well as the money. I was in town (Caro) one day to buy some things, one of which was a pair of shoes for myself. Stopping by the J.C. Penney store, where we usually shopped for shoes and clothes, I found the pair that I wanted and took them to the counter. I reached for my wallet to pay for the shoes, and at that moment realized I had forgotten to bring along my ration stamp.

Now, some of you younger folks might be thinking, "So what's the big deal?" Well, the big deal is, that you might have had a pocket full of $20 dollar bills with you, but if you couldn't come up with a ration stamp, you went home without the shoes. So, I told the clerk my dilemma, and said I would be sure to bring the stamp in the next time I came to town. With a look of skepticism, she turned and walked over to speak to the store owner, Arthur Gieb.

In just a moment, he came over and asked me what my Dad's name was, and I told him, Will Smith. Without any hesitation, he turned to the clerk and said, "He's as good as the Treasury Department." Wow!! I walked out of the store that day feeling like a million dollars. No, not because I had my new shoes, but because I had something money couldn't buy--a Pa who was as good as his word. Maybe you think that didn't do something for this eighteen-year-old boy. But Mr. Gieb had just put into words what our family, as well as others in the community knew--our Pa was a man of integrity!

For the first several months of 1941, Pa had not been feeling too well and had begun to slow down because of a heart condition. He said that it bothered him to ride the tractor over the rough ground. It was then that I tried to be a little more selective in the work that I called on him to do. Little by little, I took over most of the physical work-related responsibilities on the farm. When Pa began to realize that he probably would not recover from his illness, he began to make some arrangements for the well-being of the family.

Although my three younger brothers were old enough now to do a considerable amount of the work on the farm, there was still going to be an added responsibility fall on my shoulders. My brother, John, who was eight years older than myself, was working in Birmingham, near Detroit. Pa called him home one weekend and asked him if he might consider leaving his job there, and move back home to help me with the farm. He said that he would.

I'm sure I didn't realize at the time what a sacrifice that would be for John and his family. He gave up a very good job in order to honor the wishes of his Pa and, in so doing, was a tremendous help to me.

Pa was under Dr. Theron Donahue's care for a period of time, but his condition continued to worsen. On March 22, 1942, at age 59, Pa passed away in our home with most of the family nearby.

He was survived by his wife, Susanna; his thirteen children, Alvin, Elden, Roy, Mabel, John, Mary, Rosella, Ruth, William, Pearl, Fred, Richard, and Donald; and eleven grandchildren ages ranging from eight down to two, Kathryn, Marilyn, Theron, David, Wayne, June, Lowell, Ronald, William, James, and Naomi Jean.

He didn't quite make it to three score and ten, but the impact of his righteous life lives on in his descendants. I can say as one who was near him during the closing days of his life, I don't think I ever heard him complain about his condition even once.

Soon after this, John, Ruth, and their family moved back home. The house on the gravel farm was empty at that time, so they moved in there. John and I got along extremely well working in partnership that year. Along with the work, we also managed to squeeze in time for fishing and hunting--pheasants as well as deer.

Rationing was still in force, which made it more complicated when we needed such things as tires, batteries, and fuel for the equipment.

One day along about the middle of October, John and I were out in the field just north of the barn with pitchforks, turning over bunches (small piles of navy bean plants) so they would dry out faster. Howard and Lola Remington lived a 1/2 west and 1/4 of a mile north of us. As we were working along, I faintly heard Howard's tractor start up. Naturally, I didn't think anymore about it because there was nothing unusual about that. But about twenty minutes later I thought I faintly heard a scream for help. I said to John, "I believe Howard is in trouble, maybe we had better go and see." So, we ran to the house, got in the car, and raced over to the Remington's.

When we drove in the yard, Lola was just helping Howard into the house, hobbling along on one foot. What had happened was, he had connected his tractor up to his combine to get it ready to thresh beans. On the front of the combine, there were two canvas aprons that ran together to carry the grain or beans up and into the cylinder. The problem was, he had put the power shaft in gear and was standing up on top of the machine. The top canvas became stuck and was not turning as it should. So, he gave it a kick, and the moment his foot hit the top roller, it started turning again, pulling his right foot into the whirling cylinders. It all happened in an instant!

Even though the fore-part of his foot was mashed, he was still able to get down from the machine, and with his wife's help, also make it into the house. She quickly bandaged his foot as best she could, and after assisting him into the back seat of our car, we rushed him to the Cass City Hospital.

Later, Lola asked us how we knew they needed help. We told her that we thought we had heard him holler soon after his tractor started up. She was so thankful that we had come. This family had endured many difficult situations during the previous years, and unfortunately, Howard never did really recover from this incident.

Five

Tattered Tent Roof

As the deer season approached in the year of 1942, John and I had already decided to hunt in a different location from where the rest of our usual party was hunting. They were planning to go to Hubbard Lake again, but we thought we would go up near Mio and Lazurne.

So we took our farm truck and put the stock rack on it. The rack was 8 x 12 and our tent was just the right size to set down over the rack. We put a heavy piece of carpeting on the floor and built in a couple bunks for sleeping. The day before the season opened, we got all our gear together; which included, heavy woolen hunting clothes, blankets, guns, shells, gas lantern, extra gasoline, etc., and loaded it all into our new living quarters. Boy, it sure was cozy!

Wow! What fun it was making the final plans for another trip into the north woods. Even the mention of the woods stirs something inside a hunter. On the morning of November 14th, the sky was overcast with a slight tingle in the air as John and I pulled out of the yard with our hunting camp on wheels. It was good to be free of the farm work for a few days. As we came into Bay City, we were both ready to stop for breakfast. While we were enjoying our eggs, bacon, toast, and coffee, we sorta mapped out our hunting strategy.

The area around Mio and Lazurne had always been known as excellent deer hunting country, rated very high for the concentration of big game, but this would be our first time there. As our '38 Chevy hunting cabin rolled down U. S. Highway 23 north of Standish, I began to visualize myself standing out on a well-worn deer trail back in among the scrub oak, miles from the nearest town.

Not far east from Mio, we found a little dirt road leading back into dense evergreens. It was late in the afternoon, so after setting up camp we walked out around just to get a feel for the new territory. There were deer tracks everywhere, but the season would not be open until sunup the next day.

Back at camp we lit the cook stove, whipped us up some supper, and then sat back on our bunks and reminisced about other hunting trips he and I had taken together. We laughed about the time we had been hunting in the Hubbard Lake area when the forest ranger came by and enlisted us into helping them fight a big fire up in the hills south of the lake. I'm telling you we were both ready for the sack after flogging the forest floor for two hours that warm November afternoon. But we had some good laughs over it anyway.

Before we crawled in for the night, we opened the back door of our camper and just stood there for a few seconds breathing in the exhilarating smells of the great-out-of-doors. It was a nice, light feeling being miles away from the cares of the work-a-day world back on the farm.

The next morning we were up at the crack of dawn fixing breakfast. It was a little too warm for good hunting the first day, so we spent quite a bit of time just slowly walking through the big woods. We soon realized that this was no place for us, because we had come across several big doe that had been shot illegally, and left laying on the ground. We just didn't feel good about what we were experiencing. So along about the middle of the afternoon, we decided to leave that area and head out toward Hubbard Lake where the other guys were. We would have about a thirty or forty mile drive and the roads were not good. Many places the tree limbs hung very low over the road which was extremely narrow. We just sorta took our time driving back across this wilderness area.

Soon after we got out on the road, a light, cold rain began falling. About halfway to our destination, we came to a little old country store way out in the sticks. We decided to stop and inquire about the road ahead. It was now pitchdark and raining when we stepped out of the truck. John walked around behind and opened the tailgate door. As it swung open, he looked up into our living quarters and couldn't believe his eyes. He could look right up through the roof of our tent. The low hanging tree limbs along the dirt roads had done a number on our nice cabin. Our tent roof was ripped to shreds, and our bunks along with our clothes and bedding were already wet from the rain.

Now what? We were sorta stymied for a little while, but then a brilliant idea came to us. We decided to take the carpet up off the floor and drape it over the tent roof. That worked out fine with just a little ingenuity. We were able to buy some roofing nails and a few pieces of lath at the store to hold the carpet in place. It wasn't completely waterproof, but we made it the rest of the way to Hubbard Lake.

We came trudging up to their cabin about 10:30 that night. After telling them our plight, they gladly welcomed us in for the duration of the week. Hunting was not exceptionally good in that area, but it was lots of fun being all together again.

Six

Just Who Was That Beauty?

Now I want to back up a few months to the second week in August of '42. It was not normal for me to be attending the Annual Conference of the United Brethren Church at Carson City. To be perfectly honest, I don't know why I went that year. It may have been specifically to take my Ma and sister, Ruthie, because she had to help in the dining hall that Sunday.

It was around lunch time, so I wandered over to the hall, which was in the basement of the adult dormitory. From the outside entrance to the basement you had to go down five or six steps. So I opened the door and started down when all of a sudden something caught my eye. Right in plain view, about half way across the room, making her way along between the long tables, was the most beautiful young lady I had ever seen. She wore a cinnamon colored satin-like dress, and high-heeled shoes.

I thought, *Wow! I wonder who she is? I must get the full scoop on that doll.* I'd never seen her before as far as I knew. So, I began to inquire around a little and learned that she was Marian Bryde, the daughter of one of the preachers. I had always been sorta shy, so had not dated anyone up until then. But things were beginning to transpire that changed everything!

This happened to be the Sunday of the Annual Conference, when each of the pastors found out where they would be stationed for the coming year. They were not at liberty to choose where they would go each time. That decision was made for them by a stationing committee consisting of the bishop of the conference and the district superintendent. They based their decision on information gathered from the delegates from each individual field.

Now I began thinking to myself, *Wouldn't it be neat if the Bryde family would be sent to the Colwood Church this year. Yes, that would be just ducky, but maybe that's pushing my luck too far. But....*

During the conference session, I sat with a keen interest, waiting for the stationing committee's report to be read. That in itself was weird because normally I couldn't have cared less who went where. But I just knew the committee had the mind of the Lord when they compiled that list, because when the bishop read down through it and came to our church, he said, "Colwood, W.T. Bryde." That was sure music to my ears. As they say, *that just made my day.* I wasn't overly concerned whether he was a good preacher or not because I know, at times, you can't have everything.

The normal custom was for the new pastor to be at his next assignment the Sunday following the Annual Conference. And unbeknown to me, my Ma had done what she and Pa had done many times in the previous years, and that was to invite the new preacher and his family over for dinner on that first Sunday. Now are you beginning to see the pieces falling into place? How lucky could I get? I haven't the slightest idea what Rev. Bryde's message was that day or how I sized him up--I must have been thinking about something else.

Marian at agie 19

It was on the way to church that morning when Ma told us that she had invited the Bryde's for dinner. I thought, *How nice!* After church when I brought the rest of our family home, I knew that in just a short while a 1937 Plymouth would arrive with Rev. and Mrs. Bryde, Marian and Leslie.

I guess I must have heard their car coming, because I hiked out and stood behind the wood shed so that I could watch without being seen. I know that this sounds very strange to most of you, but I honestly don't remember another thing about that day. The last thing I remember was that black Plymouth and the little cloud of dust, as Rev. Bryde whipped it around the circle drive and stopped at the front door. I guess my mind must have just gone blank. However, I did come to my senses shortly afterward and began to do a little scheming, but it would be several months before I got real serious.

Seven

Blackouts

Our country was soon to be involved in a war on two fronts: against Germany and Japan. For the past few years blackouts had been pretty common in big cities such as London and Paris. Let me explain what a blackout is: If the military advisors or government officials believed that an enemy attack was imminent, they would sound an alarm, and every house, office, business establishment, etc., would turn all their lights out. This was done to confuse incoming aircraft as to where the key targets were. This had been a very real issue in western Europe and Great Britain for many months.

Although our country was never attacked during this period, the government did initiate blackouts, or air raid warning drills. They appointed captains, or wardens, to be responsible for certain geographical areas. These drill were carried out every so often as preparation measures in case our country was threatened by an attack from the air. My brother, Elden, was at the Colwood store, which would have been the summer of '42, and they appointed him warden over several square miles in the Colwood vicinity.

He coordinated the drills, but there were others appointed to help carry out the plan. He asked me if I would be responsible for the area we lived in. My territory was one mile wide and two miles long. This is the way it worked. The drills were held in the evening between 7 - 9 p.m., depending on the time of year. Each of us would be informed by phone in advance as to the exact time to begin. So, at the appointed time, I, with my sister, Pearl, would climb into our '39 Olds. (Pearl and I being near the same age and enjoying each others company, often did things together, such as attending parties and school functions. This was just another one of those times that we could be together.) We would head out to contact every home on our one by two mile route. A few of the homes on our list were Roy Vader, Howard Remington, Charles Dibbley, Clyde Rhodes, Uncle Ed Dillon, John Matt, Lee Dillon, Uncle Steve Dillon, Uncle Tom Smith, Jim Cross, Carl Smith, and Willie Bryde.

We stopped out in front of every home and lightly tapped the horn. That was their signal to turn off every light on their property and leave them off for a given length of time. As soon as we saw their lights begin to go out, we would zoom on to our next house, and so on, until we had covered every home in the area. I sorta enjoyed that little exercise, as it made me feel important, realizing I was being of service to my country.

Eight

A New Beginning

It wasn't long after this that I began to get up nerve enough to bug my sister, Pearl, about asking Marian Bryde if she would like to go with us to the various activities. Somewhere in the back of my mind I knew that before long I would have to take the bull by the horns and do my own inviting. Sure enough, the day finally came.

Our church (Colwood United Brethren) had what was called a Christian Endeavor business meeting once a month in someone's home. They would have a short business session, then the remainder of the evening would be for games, social times, and food. I believe it was on one such meeting that Marian and I had our first official date.

We enjoyed each other's company, and during the last few months of her senior year of high school, 1943, we became very serious about our relationship to each other. This was also the second year that John and I farmed together. John and his family had moved to the Dettweiler farm east of Colwood, and we were still on the Kerridge farm.

In the fall of 1943 the Kerridge farm was sold, and we auctioned off our farm equipment to settle Pa's estate. Soon thereafter our family moved up on the gravel farm, south of Colwood. I mean all of us who were still at home with mother: Pearl, Fred, Dick, Don and I. Ruth was not married, but was at Big Laurel Mission in Kentucky at the time. Right after Christmas that year, Marian and I were engaged. On February 23, 1944, we were married in the Colwood United Brethren Church with her Dad performing the ceremony.

I had bought a small house trailer, which we took on our honeymoon up in northern Michigan. The first night we were there, we woke up in the morning to about eight to ten inches of new snow on the ground--sure was beautiful!

We spent most of a week there, and upon coming home, parked our trailer in the yard at Ma's place on the Colwood Road out next to the barn. We made it our home for that summer while I farmed the eighty acres across the road, which was owned by Charlie Calbury.

A few days after we got back from our wedding trip, my brother, John and his wife, Ruth, had a reception for us at their house. We had a wonderful time and received many nice gifts. One of those gifts was a six place setting of china that is occupying a place of honor in our china cabinet yet today.

That winter was very cold with lots of snow. It was a custom for a newly married couple to be treated to a shivaree by their "friends." For the benefit of the younger folks, I'll read you the definition from Webster's dictionary. "Shivaree [It comes from the word Charivari], and means 'A noisy demonstration or celebration, especially a mock serenade with, kettles, horns, etc., to a couple on their wedding night.'"

Over the years that custom was altered a little, in that, it did not always take place on the wedding night, but in most cases came several nights later when the couple least expected it. Usually one of their best friends would instigate it. In our case it was not only one of my best friends, but this good friend was also my own brother, John. He contacted all his other friends and neighbors and designated a certain night for the raid. They generally planned to strike about an hour after they figured you had gone to bed. The whole motley crew then met down the road far enough away so no one would be suspicious of anything. The list of equipment they carried included such things as shotguns, dynamite (to set off a safe distance from the buildings), old wash tubs, old brake drums, hammers, horns, and probably one of the meanest of all would be what was called a range boiler (a tall galvanized water tank with a row of big rivets the full length of it).

They leaned that tank up against the side of your house and dragged a crow bar up and down over those big rivets. You talk about a racket! Can you imagine our little house trailer enduring such an attack? Well, they all had a wonderful time surprising us, and we concluded the celebration around 11 p.m. by treating everyone to Baby Ruth candy bars.

Several nights before the shivaree, when there was still about six inches of snow on the ground and slightly crusted over, Marian and I had gone to bed but had not fallen asleep yet. While laying there talking quietly, we began to hear what sounded like somebody walking in the snow. My brother John and our cousin Lawrence Smith had decided to spy on us. They had left their car parked a couple of hundred yards away, on the side of the road. Now here they came, stealing along through the deep snow, crunch, crunch, crunch, crunch. So we peaked out through the crack in the curtain and there in the moonlight was John and Lawrence with their ear right next to our bedroom window.

After a few minutes, I guess they had decided that we were already asleep, so with much disappointment, they quietly crunched their way back out to their car and drove off. They probably were just checking to see how early we were going to bed so they would know when to plan the raid. Well, those were enjoyable years starting out into married life together.

Since then, the Lord has blessed us with two wonderful daughters. On August 27, 1945, Faye Annette was born in Cass City, Michigan. Then about six and a half years later on February 20, 1952, Yvonne Eileen was born in Highland Park, Michigan.

I can't express in words what a blessing our two daughters have been to us. They each have their own families now, and it is my hope and prayer that the Lord will allow each and every one of my descendants to experience as much enjoyment out of life as I have.